POKéMON®

DIAMOND AND PEARL

WORLD OF SINNOH

by Simcha Whitehill

ISBN-13: 978-0-545-09938-7
ISBN-10: 0-545-09938-2

Published by Scholastic Inc.

12 11 10 9 8 7 6 5 4 3 2 1 9 10 11 12 13 14/0

Designed by Dirty Bandits
Printed in the U.S.A.
First printing, January 2009

SCHOLASTIC INC.

NEW YORK TORONTO LONDON AUCKLAND SYDNEY
MEXICO CITY NEW DELHI HONG KONG BUENOS AIRES

NOW ENTERING: SINNOH

The Sinnoh Region is full of exciting things to do, places to go, and people to see! So be sure to bring this book along to guide you through the ins and outs of Sinnoh's sights. From fun facts to cool contests to Pokémon playgrounds, all the info is at your fingertips!

HERE'S WHAT YOU'LL FIND INSIDE

The Sagas of Sinnoh

Follow in Ash's, Dawn's, Brock's, and Pikachu's footsteps as they explore the region, make new friends, encounter rare types of Pokémon, and battle for ribbons and badges.

Roundup of the Regional Pokémon

Sinnoh is loaded with an amazing variety of powerful Pokémon, like the Legendary Suicune and mischievous Mismagius. With all the Pokémon knowledge in this book, you could become a professor!

Cast of Characters

Sinnoh is a colorful place, and so are the people who call it home. Get to know them — the good, the bad, and the unique.

Travel Tips

Find out how to get around Sinnoh by foot, by bicycle, by boat, or by flying Drifloon. It's all about where you want to go and how to get there!

Rivals in the Region

Get the lowdown on those willing to stoop to steal Pokémon or beat you out in a battle. From Team Rocket to Hunter J, you'll be able to spot trouble a mile away.

Expert Extras

Dig in on all the details of Sinnoh's best-kept secrets, like the Amber Castle, the Ancient Pokémon Restorers, and even where to eat!

JUST TURN THE PAGE AND START YOUR SINNOH JOURNEY!

TWINLEAF TOWN

Pokémon: Diamond and Pearl, Episode I Following a Maiden's Voyage!

Today is Dawn's tenth birthday, and that means it's time for her Pokémon journey to begin! Dawn has always dreamed of becoming a Top Coordinator like her mom. After breakfast, she says good-bye to her mother, to Glameow, and to her home in Twinleaf Town.

Dawn's first stop is Sandgem Town, where she'll pick out her first Pokémon at Professor Rowan's lab. She's making good time on her pink bicycle, but along the way, she gets lost. Luckily, Professor Rowan pulls up and leads her to his lab. But when they get there, some of the Pokémon are missing.

One of the research assistants explains that Piplup and Chimchar got in a fight. Apparently, Chimchar ate more than its fair share of Pokémon food. The fight got completely out of hand: Staraptor, Starly, Chimchar, and Piplup all ran away! Dawn, ready to start her training, offers to find and return the rebellious Pokémon to the lab.

It doesn't take Dawn long to find the Pokémon, but little does she know that the hardest part is yet to come: the runaway Pokémon don't want her help! Piplup is

TRAVEL TIP
Twinleaf Town is known for fresh air that smells so sweet, it's a real treat!

especially resistant. But when Dawn helps the Pokémon fend off Ariados, she earns their respect and some well-deserved rest.

Dawn and the Pokémon recover from their rough day on the shore of a river, where Dawn spots something magical in the water. It's a Legendary Mesprit!

After their encounter, Dawn and the Pokémon return to the lab. Professor Rowan thanks Dawn for all her help and offers her a Pokémon. Earlier in the day, she couldn't decide, but now the choice seems clear. She picks Piplup as her new pal!

As Dawn rides out of Sandgem Town, our hero, Ash, is just arriving on a ferry from Kanto. Ash is excited to step foot in Sinnoh for the first time, and he is looking forward to new adventures in a new region. But hovering above the happy scene is Team Rocket, who swoop in on their hot-air balloon and steal Pikachu.

Some welcome to Sinnoh!

PIPLUP

Type: Water

Height: 1' 04"

Weight: 11.5 lbs

Proud Piplup is a strong swimmer and a special Pokémon offered in Sinnoh. This Water-type likes to live close to the ocean and in cold climates.

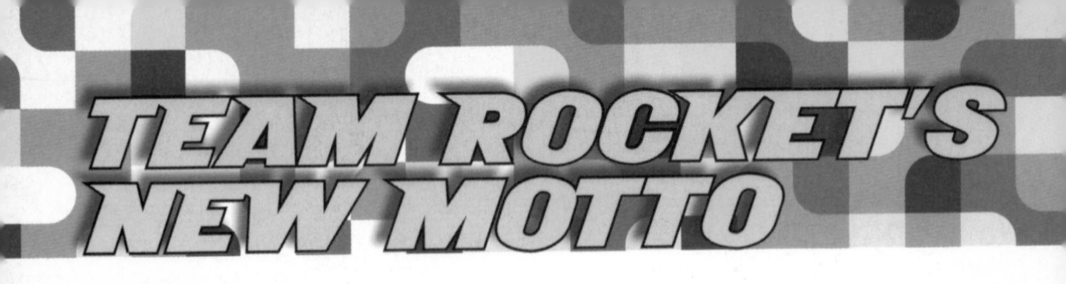

TEAM ROCKET'S NEW MOTTO

Team Rocket has never visited Sinnoh together — that is, until now. James used to spend his summers in the region, so he's Team Rocket's tour guide. Be on the lookout for their hot-air balloon, just in case they come to pick up your Pokémon as a souvenir!

While they've got a new motto, Team Rocket are still singing the same old troublesome tune. When you hear this poem, be prepared to protect your Pokémon.

Listen! Is that a voice I hear?!
It's speaking to me, loud and clear!
On the wind,
Past the stars,
In your ear!
Bringing chaos at a breakneck pace!
Dashing hope, putting fear in its place!
A rose by any other name
Is just as sweet.
When everything's worse,
Our work is complete!
Jesse!
And it's James!
Meowth, now that's a name!
Putting the do-gooders
In their place.
Team Rocket!
In your face!

SANDGEM TOWN

The seashore jewel of Sinnoh!

This town is known for its sandy beach. Be sure to stop by the local lab and visit its most renowned inhabitant, Professor Rowan.

Pokémon: Diamond and Pearl, Episode 2
Two Degrees of Separation!

Dawn and Piplup must bike to Jubilife City to compete in their first Pokémon Contest. As they travel through the woods, Dawn is on the lookout for more Pokémon. After letting a Buneary and a Burmy slip through her fingers, Dawn quickly throws a Poké Ball at a passing Pikachu. It bounces right back. That means Pikachu already belongs to someone — but who?

Just then, Team Rocket shows up to claim Pikachu. Dawn can tell they're lying. Piplup helps fight them off, and Dawn rushes the exhausted Pikachu to Nurse Joy at the Pokémon Center. When Professor Rowan checks in with the new Coordinator, she vows to return the Electric-type to its rightful Trainer, even if it means missing her first contest.

Team Rocket decides to stay at James' family's summer cottage, where he is reunited with his childhood Pokémon pal Carnivine.

Meanwhile, Aipom and Ash are searching for their lost friend Pikachu when Officer Jenny finds them. She takes Ash to Professor Rowan's lab and offers to help with the hunt, but Professor Rowan already knows where they should look. Ash sets off to meet Dawn at the Pokémon Center. On the way, a truck pulls up with a big surprise: Brock! Ash is happy to be back on the road with his buddy. Together they catch a Starly to help them locate Pikachu.

TRAVEL TIP

Biking through Sinnoh is a great way to enjoy the scenery and sights, but look out for Pikachu's Thunderbolt! It could zap away your ride.

CARNIVINE

Type: Grass

Height: 4' 07"

Weight: 59.5 lbs

The googly-eyed Grass-type Pokémon's drool may smell nice, but its mouth waters when it's going to take a bite! Avoid getting caught in Carnivine's chompers by looking out for them in their usual hang-tree branches.

Pokémon: Diamond and Pearl, Episode 3
When Pokémon Worlds Collide!

Ash and Brock are searching for Pikachu in the woods when they see a huge electric burst rise above the trees. Could it be the little yellow Electric-type they're looking for? They race toward the light and run smack into a new foe — a bad sport named Paul. And with Paul is his Elekid. He challenges Ash to a three-on-three battle, but without Pikachu, Ash isn't prepared.

Just then, a robot lumbers into view. It's Team Rocket — and they've taken Pikachu from Dawn! Piplup, Starly, and Aipom are no match for the metal machine, so Team Rocket celebrates their victory by chanting their new motto. But Ash refuses to give

TRAVEL TIP

Professor Rowan's lab in Sandgem Town is renowned for researching Pokémon evolution and the resident Pokémon of the Sinnoh Region.

up. He climbs the robot to save Pikachu while Team Rocket is busy gloating. James instructs the robot to claw Ash off, but the machine blasts Team Rocket off instead!

Officer Jenny pulls up at the scene to take the crew back to Professor Rowan's lab. There's a package waiting for Ash. It's from his mom and it has cool new outfits inside! Outside, Paul is still waiting to battle Ash. They battle, but the outcome is a tie. But Ash isn't disappointed. He has a feeling they'll meet again in Sinnoh.

Since they are all headed to Jubilife City, Dawn asks to join Brock and Ash. The boys gladly agree to travel with such a nice new friend.

Type: Electric

Height: 2' 0"

Weight: 51.8 lbs

Elekid is a walking power plant that spins its arms to create electricity. This yellow and black Electric-type's energy will shock you.

Pokémon: Diamond and Pearl, Episode 4
Dawn of a New Era

As the crew travels through the woods, Dawn tries to catch a wild Buneary. Ash tries to give her some advice, but Dawn gets flustered and the Buneary escapes. Ash and Dawn start to bicker, but suddenly, a beautiful Sunny Day Attack display brightens their mood. The Budew responsible for the light show appears with its Trainer, the wandering bard Nando. Dawn and Piplup, anxious to have their first battle, decide to challenge them. Although Budew and Nando easily beat Piplup and Dawn, Nando is encouraging. He congratulates the pair on completing their first battle and continues on his journey.

TRAVEL TIP
Late at night in the forest, if you're quiet, you can hear a chorus of wild Pokémon crooning together.

There's so much to see and do in Sinnoh. But Brock, Dawn, and Ash are responsible Trainers, so they decide that their next stop should be the Pokémon Center to visit Nurse Joy. There, Ash registers to compete in the Sinnoh League. Nurse Joy reveals that Nando can't decide whether to become a Pokémon Trainer or Coordinator.

The friends want to help Nando solve his dilemma, but it's getting dark and they still have to set up camp. When they head back into the woods, the crew stumbles upon a strange hotel. The owners insist they stay the night for free! As they all go inside, a gust of wind blows, revealing the "owners" to be Team Rocket in disguise! Piplup steps up to fight them off, but Nando and Budew jump in and make Team Rocket blast off.

Around the campfire, Ash and Dawn get in yet another fight. Peaceful poet Nando points out their squabbling is louder than the sounds of the forest Pokémon singing. Ash and Dawn apologize to each other. Ash then challenges Nando and Budew to a battle. In the middle of their fight, Budew evolves to Roselia. Although Nando and his newly grown Grass-and-Poison-type Pokémon lose to Ash and Pikachu, Nando finally decides he doesn't have to make up his mind. He will have the best of both worlds by becoming a Trainer and a Coordinator.

BUDEW

Type: Grass/Poison

Height: 0' 08"

Weight: 2.6 lbs

The Grass-and-Poison-type Pokémon likes to live near clear crystal ponds. In spring, it opens its bud and blossoms, but its beauty might make you sneeze — its buds scatter pollen.

Pokémon: Diamond and Pearl, Episode 5
Gettin' Twiggy With It!

The race is on! Ash, Brock, and Dawn chase Team Rocket, who are flying away with Pikachu. Ash calls on Starly to burst their hot-air balloon. When Pikachu lands, a wild Turtwig releases it from its net. Turtwig blasts off Team Rocket just as Ash, Dawn, and Brock catch up. But the little Pokémon thinks the friends are part of the Pokémon poaching team, so it attacks them, too. Its Razor Leaf hits a nearby Oddish, who knocks Ash and Pikachu out with its sleep powder. Turtwig then runs off with the napping Pikachu.

When Ash wakes up, he sets out to find the pair in the forest. It isn't long before he sees Pikachu, but Turtwig tackles him. Pikachu explains that Ash is his best friend. Turtwig is embarrassed, but Ash thanks it for being so nice to his Pikachu.

Trouble still awaits: Team Rocket are spying on them from their submarine. Team Rocket imprisons Turtwig and Pikachu in a waterproof glass tube. Piplup and Ash dive into the water after them, and Piplup tries to peck through the glass tube. Fortunately, Ash saves the day. He has Pikachu blast them out of the water with Iron Tail.

Now free, Turtwig head-butts Team Rocket good-bye. Then the little Pokémon lets Ash know it wants to join the crew on their journey. Excited for a new fighter and friend, Ash welcomes Turtwig to the family!

TURTWIG

Type: Grass Height: 1' 04"
Weight: 22.5 lbs

Turtwig is a Grass-type Pokémon with two leaves on top of its head. Water makes the shell on its back grow even stronger.

BEWILDER FOREST

Pokémon: Diamond and Pearl, Episode 6
Different Strokes for Different Blokes

While Brock, Dawn, and Ash prepare lunch in the woods, Piplup takes a wild Mankey's fruit. Just as Turtwig breaks up the ensuing brawl, Paul shows up. After he insults Turtwig, Ash is ready to battle.

TRAVEL TIP
When you're traveling through Bewilder Forest, be on the lookout for Pokémon. Many of them live in the woods.

Right when Turtwig is about to strike, it gets caught in Team Rocket's net. Paul, Ash, Chimchar, and Pikachu blast the bad guys off — but Paul doesn't stick around. When Ash chases after Paul to thank him, he accidentally follows him into Bewilder Forest.

Wild Stantler surround them and use their antlers to tantalize Turtwig and Ash into thinking they're in other places: in a hot desert, up in the clouds — anywhere but where they really are. Paul catches a Stantler to scare the rest off, but he doesn't hold onto his catch. To him, the Stantler isn't good enough.

Turtwig and Ash have bonded over their experience in the woods. But things go awry when Ash runs away from an approaching Stantler only to hit a tree full of Beedrill. Next a wild Ursaring arrives. It scares the Beedrill away, but it's ready to fight the crew of intruders.

While Pikachu tries to battle the towering Ursaring, Paul and Chimchar return and capture it. When Ash thanks Paul for helping them out again, Paul calls Ash a loser. Angry, Ash challenges Paul to another battle, but Chimchar beats Turtwig again! Paul takes one last chance to make fun of Ash before leaving. But Ash knows he'll see the arrogant Trainer again — and next time, Paul won't win.

ON THE ROAD

Pokémon: Diamond and Pearl, Episode 7
Like It or Lup It

Dawn and Piplup are hard at work practicing a new combination: Spin with BubbleBeam.

Meanwhile, Team Rocket has stumbled upon some berries and decided to steal the food stash. When Poliwhirl, Golduck, Whooper, and Quagsire find their pile is missing, they blame three passersby — a bunch of Ludicolo.

Team Rocket wants to poach the Ludicolo, so they pretend to be judges to try the Pokémon's case. The Ludicolo fall in love with Team Rocket when they take their side, and they use Carnivine and Seviper to fend off the other Pokémon.

As the group of Pokémon plaintiffs run away, they bump into Piplup. Golduck explains their situation and Piplup decides to help defend them. Ash, Brock, and Dawn show up, too, but Team Rocket snatches all the Pokemon, except Piplup, who continues to fight. The Water-type stuns everyone with a Spin and Bubble Beam combination so strong it sinks Team Rocket's submarine. Piplup's hard work finally paid off! Pikachu blasts the bumbling poachers right out of the sub.

Once Golduck and its friends see the Ludicolo weren't responsible for the missing meals, the Pokémon shoot Water-type attacks at Jesse, James, and Meowth. Then they all celebrate with a big berry feast.

TRAVEL TIP
There are plenty of wild berries to pick along the road in the Sinnoh Region. Pack a basket and some napkins so you're prepared to handle all the juicy bites!

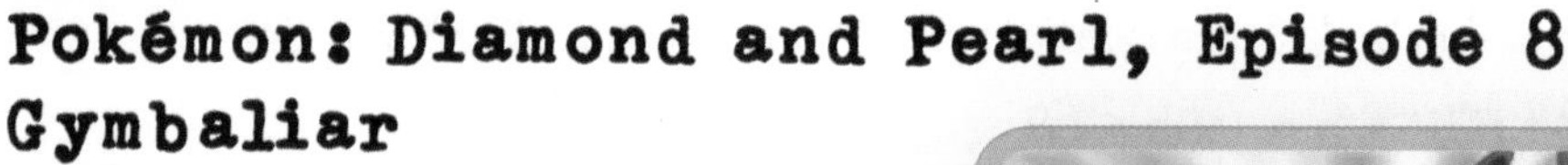

ON THE ROAD

Pokémon: Diamond and Pearl, Episode 8
Gymbaliar

While traveling, Ash, Pikachu, Brock, and Dawn meet a giant flying Scizor and its new Trainer, Minnie. She leads them to a gym palace in the middle of the woods. Princess Power Zone, who is really Jesse in disguise, greets them and offers to have James referee their battle.

Eager to earn their first gym badge together, Scizor and Minnie take her challenge. Jesse decides to battle with Croagunk, a Pokémon that followed Meowth home from the supermarket. After she cheats and wins, Jesse offers to take Scizor and train it.

TRAVEL TIP

Battlers beware, Team Rocket runs the Power Zone Gym and their badges are bogus bottle caps!

Now it's Ash's turn to battle Princess Power Zone. Jesse and Meowth insist the Gym Leader gets to choose the Pokémon. Jesse picks Pikachu, and then Team Rocket traps Pikachu in a net. Team Rocket blasts off in their hot-air balloon, taking dozens of other Trainers' Poké Balls with them — including Minnie's Scizor. The crew runs after them, and Ash calls on Starly, who deflates their getaway.

With Pikachu, Scizor, and the other Pokémon freed, Minnie decides she'll stick around and give all the other Trainers their stolen Pokémon back. As for the Croagunk, Brock offers to take care of the cheeky chap, and it happily joins their journey.

CROAGUNK

Type: Poison/Fighting

Height: 2' 04" Weight: 50.7 lbs

Croagunk might have cute chubby cheeks, but don't pinch them — they're toxic! This Poison-and-Fighting-type Pokémon can also sting you with its fingers, so don't let it pinch you either!

ON THE ROAD

Pokémon: Diamond and Pearl, Episode 9
Setting the World on Its Buneary

It's breakfast time, but Dawn won't come out of her tent. Piplup uses BubbleBeam to cure her bed head. Then Aipom jokingly runs off with Ash's hat, so Pikachu chases it into the road. Luckily, a wild Buneary saves it from hitting Officer Jenny as she races by on her motorcycle.

Buneary hops away, leaving both Ash and Dawn wishing they'd caught it. So when the wild Pokémon shows up later that day, they both jump at the opportunity. Piplup tries to battle Buneary, but gets lost in its Dizzy Punch. When Pikachu steps up to the plate, Buneary falls hard — in love, not in battle. Buneary uses Ice Beam to freeze Ash, Brock, and Dawn so it can run away with its crush.

Unfortunately, Team Rocket catches Buneary in the robot they built with stolen parts, the Sinnoh Rabble Rouser Mark III. Pikachu, worried about its new friend, makes a deal with Team Rocket! But, of course, Team Rocket keeps both Pokémon locked up.

Luckily, Croagunk catches up with its frozen friends and frees Ash, Brock, and Dawn. They rush to stop Team Rocket, but Pikachu has already used its tail to bust itself and Buneary out of the glass cages. Team Rocket knows it's time to blast off again, but Buneary freezes their rockets.

Now Dawn and Piplup battle for Buneary's friendship. Lo and behold, Dawn catches her first Pokémon!

BUNEARY

Type: Normal Height: 1' 04"

Weight: 12.1 lbs

Buneary may look soft and fluffy, but behind all the puff beats the heart of a champion battler. The Normal-type Pokémon has cute fluffy ears that it uses to sense danger and slam opponents.

JUBILIFE CITY

A big city bundle of joy!

The largest hub in Sinnoh, Jubilife City is always hustling and bustling with business, so it's a pleasure to visit!

JUBILIFE CITY

Pokémon: Diamond and Pearl, Episode 10
Not on My Watch Ya Don't!

Ash, Pikachu, Brock, and Dawn have reached Jubilife City, where Dawn plans on entering her first Pokémon Contest. All over town, there are advertisements for the new Pokétch wristwatches, and Dawn is dying for one of her own. But a store clerk tells her all the Pokétchs have been pulled from the market.

Then Ash spots three clowns selling Pokétchs on the street. The clowns give Dawn, Ash, and Brock free Pokétchs, but it turns out the peddlers are actually Team Rocket in disguise! When a Shinx won't stop crying at them, its Trainer, a younger boy named Landis, says it's because their new Pokétchs are fake. He takes them to meet his father, the inventor of Pokétchs, who complains he had to pull his product from the market because of fakes.

TRAVEL TIP
While you're in Jubilife City, pay the Pokétch inventor a visit and he'll give you a free Pokémon friendship reading!

Later that night, they notice a parade of Pokémon in a trance wandering out of the city. All the Pokémon have been lured into a storage box by Team Rocket, who have hypnotized them with a Psyduck sound embedded in their fake Pokétchs.

As they blast off with the box full of Pokémon, Dawn has Buneary freeze Team Rocket. The box bursts open, freeing all the Pokémon!

Thanks to her clever rescue plan, Dawn is rewarded with a real Pokétch of her very own. She's still nervous about her first Pokémon Contest, but at least she'll be on time!

Pokémon: Diamond and Pearl, Episode II
Mounting a Coordinator Assault

Dawn is hoping to win her first ribbon at Jubilife City's Pokémon Contest, but her necklace is missing! Just then, a Glameow strolls up with her choker looped through its tail. Its Trainer, Zoey, introduces herself and wishes Dawn luck in her very first competition.

After Aipom does a Stunning Star display, Dawn encourages Ash to enter the contest, too. They both register and are given special Sinnoh Contest Coordinator Passes, a ribbon case, a clear Poké Ball capsule, and seals that give every Pokémon a grand fireworks-filled entrance.

Tricky Team Rocket is lurking at the contest, too. While Jesse pretends to be pig-tailed Trainer Jesselina, James and Meowth decide to sell fake seals to unsuspecting buyers.

The day of her contest debut, Dawn is so nervous, she has a hard time getting ready to perform. Zoey gives her a little help and a little hairspray.

During Round One, Zoey wows the judges with Misdreavus, Ash astounds with Aipom, Jesselina sneaks by with Carnivine, and Dawn puts on a show with Piplup. The competition is stiff and the Jubilife City Contest must continue. . . .

TRAVEL TIP

In front of the Jubilife City Stadium is a Pokémon shopper's paradise! The awesome outdoor marketplace has plenty of cool things to buy, as long as the sellers aren't Team Rocket.

MISDREAVUS

Type: Ghost

Height: 2' 04"

Weight: 2.2 lbs

A Ghost-type Pokémon, Misdreavus' moves will haunt you! It loves to cause trouble invisibly, but its scary screech always gives it away.

Pokémon: Diamond and Pearl, Episode 12 Arrival of a Rival

It's time for Round Two of the competition. Zoey, Dawn, Ash, and Team Rocket's undercover contestant, Jesselina, are all still in it to win it!

Backstage, Ash mentions to Zoey that he's trying to win the Sinnoh League by showing off his sparring skills, but he entered the Jubilife City Contest because Aipom begged him. On stage, Zoey and Glameow defeat Ash and Aipom in battle by playing a strong defense. Ash congratulates Zoey and she suggests showy Aipom would be in better hands with a Coordinator like Dawn — who is up next!

TRAVEL TIP

Jubilife City is named for the joy it brings both visitors and residents. Who wouldn't want to call such a happy place home?

Buneary and Dawn try to ice out Glameow, but Zoey fires up some moves and cooks the new Coordinator. After her loss, Dawn calls her mother for comfort. Johanna reminds Dawn that she must stay strong and lean on her friends because she is just starting out.

Back at the contest, Glameow easily beats Jesselina and Carnivine, proving yet again that Zoey is an amazing Coordinator. She has won the Jubilife City Ribbon and inspired Dawn. Dawn congratulates Zoey on her success and says she someday hopes to be good enough to beat her new friend.

GLAMEOW

Type: Normal
Height: 1' 08"
Weight: 8.6 lbs.
Agile and alluring, this Pokémon is easily identified by its long curly tail. While Normal-type Glameow makes a nice companion, it can claw, scratch, and whack you with its tail.

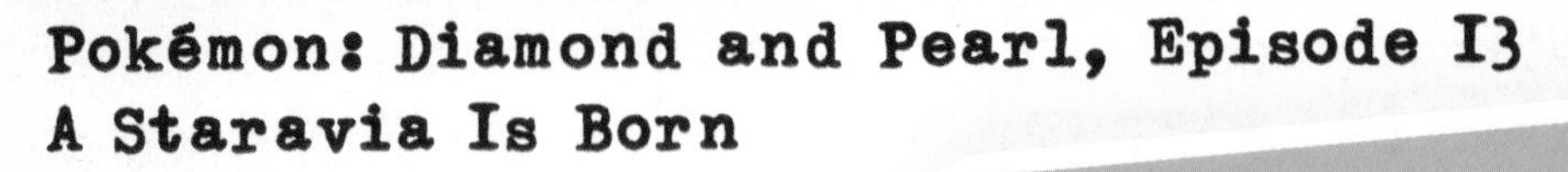

Pokémon: Diamond and Pearl, Episode 13
A Staravia Is Born

Ash and Starly are practicing for their first big competition when the little Normal-and-Flying-type injures its leg. While Brock bandages Starly, the pretty protector of the local Pokémon, Rosebay, distracts him. Rosebay has a big problem — a lot of the bird Pokémon in the area are missing. Naturally, Ash, Dawn, and Brock volunteer to help find them.

TRAVEL TIP

Many species of Flying-type Pokémon live in the forest around the Valley Path. Be sure to bring your binoculars and keep your eyes on the sky!

Ash sends Starly to look around, but when it doesn't return, Rosebay leads them to a popular place for Pokémon, the Valley Path. There they discover a hideout with a huge net set by Team Rocket. Ash sends Pikachu to round up the forest Pokémon to destroy it.

Meanwhile, Meowth is preparing to take hundreds of captured Pokémon to the boss, Giovanni. A Hoothoot hypnotizes Meowth to set them free instead. The Pokémon are able to escape — all except Starly.

Just in time, Pikachu flies in on a Pidgeon with all the forest's flying Pokémon in tow. Together, the bird Pokémon destroy the net, but Team Rocket still tries to put up a fight.

In battle, Starly surprises everyone as it evolves into a Staravia. Using Aerial Ace, Staravia blasts Team Rocket off. Now Ash is even more excited to take his pal to their first competition in Sinnoh in Oreburgh City!

STARLY

Type: Normal/Flying

Height: 1' 0"

Weight: 4.4 lbs

Known for its strong, small wings and big beak, you can hear Starly's chitchat coming a mile away. Starly is a great pal to have up in the air and on the lookout.

ON THE ROAD

Pokémon: Diamond and Pearl, Episode 14
Leave It to Brocko!

A whole colony of Seedot and its evolved forms, Nuzleaf and Shiftry, live in a thousand-year-old tree. One night, a Nuzleaf accidentally fell onto a Vileplume that carried it off into the woods. When Nuzleaf woke up, Nurse Joy was trying to help it, but it was still afraid.

Brock, Ash, Dawn, and Pikachu are on their way to Oreburgh City when they see the Pokémon attacking Nurse Joy out of fear. Brock and Bonsly soothe the scared Nuzleaf, and Ash volunteers to bring it back home. Their task gets tougher when a couple of mountain climbers, who are actually Team Rocket in disguise, claim that the Nuzleaf is their Shiftry's missing best friend.

When Dawn pulls out her Pokédex, she discovers the Shiftry is none other than Meowth in a white wig, but it's too late. Team Rocket has nabbed both Nuzleaf and Bonsly. Brock jumps on their getaway hot-air balloon, but he still can't stop Team Rocket. Ash and Staravia get shut out by Seviper, and Brock is taken hostage, too.

TRAVEL TIP

The way to warm a Nuzleaf's heart is to cover your mouth with a leaf, then blow on it like a harmonica. The sweet sound would make anyone smile, but especially this Grass-and-Dark-type Pokémon.

BONSLY

Type: Rock Height: 1' 08"

Weight: 33.1 lbs

Don't let its brown body fool you. Bonsly is actually a Rock-type Pokémon and those three green balls on its head are really rocks.

Deep in the woods, Team Rocket ties Brock to a tree, but he cleverly offers to cook them dinner. As they're eating, Brock runs off with the cage of captured Pokémon. Baby Bonsly is then able to bust them out, but it takes so much strength Bonsly evolves into a Sudowoodo.

However, Team Rocket catches up with them while they are crossing a river. Seviper and Carnivine fight Brock and Croagunk, but it's Sudowoodo who saves the day by conquering its fear of water and continuing to fight off Team Rocket.

Ash, Dawn, and Pikachu aren't the only ones to notice there's a battle going on. A Shiftry from the thousand-year-old tree arrives to help its fellow Pokémon friends. The Shiftry slashes Team Rocket's balloon and then Pikachu blasts them off.

The crew hugs Nuzleaf goodbye. It's happy to have found its way home, and the crew is ready to get back on the road to Oreburgh City, where Ash will have his first gym battle in Sinnoh!

THE THOUSAND-YEAR-OLD TREE

Home to a huge colony of Seedot, Nuzleaf, and Shiftree, this giant tree is over ten times the age of your great grandma, but it is still growing bigger, taller, stronger, and even older every day.

OREBURGH CITY

A diamond in the rough!

Rock and roll into this mining town with mountains full of fossils, coal, and gemstone treasure.

OREBURGH CITY GYM

Pokémon: Diamond and Pearl, Episode 15
The Shape of Things to Come

Ash, Brock, Dawn, and Pikachu arrive at the Oreburgh City gym, but Paul, the bad sport, has beaten them there. Ian, who cares for the Pokémon at the gym, informs them that they'll both have to wait for Roark, the Gym Leader, to finish his work at the coal mines before the battle for badges can begin. Roark is a real Rock-type Pokémon fanatic! He has dedicated his gym to Rock-type Pokémon and he spends his free team using a special machine to find Pokémon fossils for the museum.

When Roark returns, he finds Paul ready to battle. Despite the Gym Leader's raring to go Rock-type Pokémon, Geodude, Onix, and Cranidos, Paul wins with Azumarill, Chimchar, and Elekid. Roark, Ash, Dawn, and Brock are all impressed with Paul's skill and he is proud to receive the prestigious Coal Badge from the Oreburgh Gym.

Up next, it's Ash's turn to battle for his first gym badge in Sinnoh!

TRAVEL TIP

Oreburgh City is known for the treasures, from fossils to gemstones, discovered in its local mines.

CRANIDOS

Type: Rock

Height: 2' 11"

Weight: 69.4 lbs

Cranidos roamed the jungles of Sinnoh hundreds of millions of years ago, but scientists who found a fossil of the Pokémon saved it from extinction. This ancient Rock-type Pokémon has a rock-hard skull and it's not afraid to butt into a battle!

Pokémon: Diamond and Pearl, Episode 16
A Gruff Act to Follow

Ash has been waiting patiently to battle the Oreburgh Gym Leader, Roark. Paul was already able to win the gym's coveted Coal Badge, but he's still being a bad sport. He calls Ash pathetic, doesn't even remember who Dawn is, and then gives away the Azumarill that lost a round. Ash wants to show Paul that being a good friend makes you a great Trainer, but unfortunately, after a long match, Roark, Cranidos, and Onix defeat Aipom, Turtwig, Pikachu, and Ash.

And then there's more bad news. While the crew is busy at the gym, Team Rocket has been plotting their next move right around the corner at the Oreburgh Mining Museum. Kenzo, a research assistant, mistook the terrible trio for famous Pokémon professors and showed them the three machines the museum scientists use to bring fossilized Pokémon back to life.

Team Rocket is plotting to use the technology for evil, but will Ash get there before they get their greedy paws on any prehistoric Pokémon?

TRAVEL TIP

Make sure you swing by the Oreburgh Mining Museum to see all the rare Pokémon fossils, some of which were found locally by Roark, the Gym Leader. The museum is also home to one of the largest Pokémon research facilities.

ONIX

Type: Rock/Ground

Height: 28' 10" Weight: 463.0 lbs

Onix is a Rock-and-Ground-type Pokémon that can tunnel through soil at fifty mph! While it may go fast as a car, it doesn't need a map to know where it going. A magnet in its head gives it directions.

Pokémon: Diamond and Pearl, Episode 17
Wild in the Streets

Ash and the Pokémon are practicing for a rematch with Roark in the Oreburgh Coal Mine. Brock offers Ash a practice battle with Sudowoodo, since it uses Double-Edge like Roark's Onix.

TRAVEL TIP

Oreburgh City is home to three fossil restoration machines, which rejuvenate ancient Pokémon in a mere twenty-four hours. So if you've dug up a stone specimen, bring it by the research center and watch it come to life!

Meanwhile, Team Rocket is hiding in the woods with a fossil restorer they've just stolen. A rejuvenated Aerodactyl pops out of the machine, fights off the terrible trio, and then heads straight for Oreburgh City.

Dawn is going to town to find out more about the next Pokémon Contest in Floaroma Town, but her visit gets interrupted when the Aerodactyl starts attacking the city! It's on a rampage, and not even Kabutops and Armaldo, the other ancient Pokémon at the research center, can stop it. So Cranidos steps up to take a shot, but Team Rocket sneaks up in a robot made out of the fossil restorer machine and greedily grabs Kabutops and Armaldo.

Luckily, the enraged Aerodactyl busts them free from Team Rocket's robot, however, it is still terrorizing the town. Dawn has Buneary and Piplup join forces to ground the prehistoric Pokémon. Finally, the research team from the museum is able to put all three ancient Pokémon safely back in their Poké Balls.

Team Rocket tries to slip away, but their trap made Cranidos so mad, it evolves into Rampardos. It uses its newfound strength to rip apart the robot and head-butt Team Rocket until they blast off.

Ash is so impressed by the Rampardos, he challenges Roark to another gym battle!

OREBURGH CITY

Pokémon: Diamond and Pearl, Episode 18
O'er the Rampardos We Watched!

The crew is excited for Ash's rematch with Roark. Ash, Aipom, Turtwig, and Pikachu have been training even harder than usual, but will it be enough to earn Ash his first badge in the Sinnoh Region?

Roark's Cranidos was a tough competitor when they last battled, and now it's evolved into an even rougher Rampardos. So while Ash, Aipom, and Pikachu defeat Onix and Geodude using their new spinning dodge move, it's going to take one tough Turtwig to beat the hardheaded Rampardos.

Of course, Ash and his new Grass-type buddy are up to the challenge. They're happy to have their friends Dawn, Buneary, Piplup, and Brock there to cheer them on! After Ash instructs his Pokémon to use awesome and creative attacks, he defeats the remarkable Rampardos. Everyone, including Roark, is impressed with his skills. Ash is awarded his first badge in Sinnoh, the cool Coal Badge!

TRAVEL TIP

The Oreburgh City Gym is home to an amazing collection of Rock-type Pokémon and a special rocky field. So if you're off to battle Roark for a badge, make sure you're prepared for a stone-cold fight to the finish!

RAMPARDOS

Type: Rock

Height: 5' 03" Weight: 226.0 lbs

Rampardos has a skull as strong as steel and can knock over trees better than a bulldozer. This Rock-type Pokémon is hard to find because it's the evolved form of Cranidos — an ancient Pokémon that can only be resurrected through fossil restoration technology.

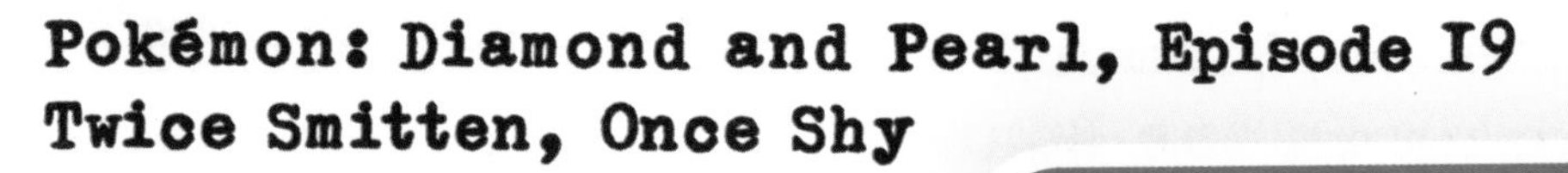

Pokémon: Diamond and Pearl, Episode 19
Twice Smitten, Once Shy

> **TRAVEL TIP**
> If a passing Pachirisu makes your hair stand on end with one of its charged zaps, you can bring it back down with water.

On a sunny afternoon in the woods, Dawn is captivated by a wild Pachirisu. At first, it's too fast for Dawn, Buneary, and Piplup to catch it, and it zaps them all. After that big burst of energy, Pachirisu is tired and Dawn picks it up with a Poké Ball. She is thrilled to start training her third Pokémon for the next contest in Floaroma Town!

However, when she takes it out, Pachirisu refuses to get back in its Poké Ball and it just won't stop zapping her. Dawn tries to set Pachirisu free, but it doesn't want to leave her side. So Dawn abandons her new chum in the woods, where Team Rocket finds it. Jesse instantly falls for the blue furball.

Meanwhile, Dawn tells Ash and Brock about her failed attempt to make Pachirisu her pal. Her buddies give her a pep talk and together they set out to find Pachirisu again.

Jesse tries to lure Pachirisu with food. However, Pachirisu just zaps the troublemaking trio. Pachirisu tries to run back into Dawn's arms, but Jesse grabs Pachirisu and Team Rocket flies off in their hot-air balloon. But the Electric-type Pokémon blasts them off. Pachirisu has rescued its new buddies and proven to be a real pal in a pinch!

PACHIRISU

Type: Electric

Height: 1' 04"

Weight: 8.6 lbs

Pachirisu is irresistibly adorable, but it's also quick-witted and quick on its feet. A handful that holds electricity in its cheeks, its silly personality and power will shock you.

ON THE ROAD

Pokémon: Diamond and Pearl, Episode 20
Mutiny in the Bounty!

TRAVEL TIP
The path to Floaroma Town is a wonderful place to pick a bouquet of beautiful wildflowers!

Ash, Brock, Dawn, and Pikachu are passing through a beautiful flower patch on their way to Floaroma Town when Hunter J swoops in on a Salamence. She zaps a gardening Gardevoir and kidnaps it in her flying tank. Melodi, Gardevoir's Trainer, screams for help, so Ash and Pikachu rush after Hunter J. She uses Ariados to tie Ash up and then J nabs Pikachu too.

Team Rocket stumbles upon the scene and is so jealous of J, they step in to fight her. But J freezes Meowth and flies off with all her stolen Pokémon. Brock, Dawn, and Officer Jenny arrive on the scene. Jenny explains that she's been trying to track down Hunter J because she's been stealing Pokémon all over Sinnoh and selling them to the highest bidder. Ash offers to help Jenny track J down, and they ask a Kirlia to use its psychic abilities to predict where J will strike next.

Officer Jenny leads them to the spot Kirlia showed them, and Hunter J is already parked there! All together, including Team Rocket, they bust in her tank to find the stolen Pokémon. Unfortunately, Drapion and J's goons catch up with them. Ash thinks fast and leads everyone out through an airshaft. Team Rocket releases Meowth and Ash saves Pikachu and Gardevoir.

Just when they think they're safe, Hunter J's tank takes to the sky and she ejects all the visitors in mid air. Luckily, Melodi calls out to Gardevoir to use Teleport to move all the people and Pokémon safely onto the ground. Hooray!

Officer Jenny arrests all the goons, but sly Hunter J still manages to get away. . . .

DRAPION
Type: Poison/Dark
Height: 4' 03"
Weight: 135.6 lbs
Look out! Drapion can turn its head 180 degrees to take in its surroundings. It uses the claws on its arms to hold onto its prey.

Pokémon: Diamond and Pearl, Episode 21
Ya See We All Want Evolution

A traveling salesman sells Team Rocket instructions for building a machine that evolves Pokémon.

Meanwhile, Ash, Brock, Dawn, and Pikachu return to Jubilife City, where they learn about the B Button League, a group for Trainers who value strength in their Pokémon without evolution. At the B Button League headquarters, they meet Haley and Oralie, sisters and leaders of the league. The girls give them a tour of their facilities, including a huge tank arena where they keep their amazing Magikarp and Feebas. Dawn is eager to see how Piplup will fare in a water battle and challenges Oralie and Magikarp.

TRAVEL TIP

The B Button League's Headquarters in Jubilife City hosts totally awesome underwater battles. But make sure you're not standing too close to the tank or you could get soaked!

Just then, the C Crystal League Shows up — but it's really Team Rocket in disguise. They sit in the stands while Dawn, Piplup, Ash, and Pikachu battle the beautiful Magikarp and Oralie. During lunchtime, Team Rocket steals Magikarp and Feebas. With the help of Staravia, they follow Team Rocket to their hideout in the woods. There, Jesse plans to put the precious Pokémon in the Pokémon evolution machine. Ash calls on Pikachu to stop the evil trio, but it gets caught in the machine too!

Thankfully, James isn't a good mechanic. Haley tells Feebas to freeze Team Rocket and Pikachu blasts them off — proving there is strength in numbers, just not necessarily in evolution.

MAGIKARP

Type: Water

Height: 2' 11"

Weight: 22.0 lbs

Magikarp are considered the weakest Pokémon of all, but this Water-type is strong enough to survive even in the most polluted rivers and lakes.

Pokémon: Diamond and Pearl, Episode 22
Borrowing on Bad Faith

On the way to Floaroma Town, Dawn hears about a village that's having a festival, and she can't wait to enter Pachirisu in its first contest. Meanwhile, Aipom is clowning around and runs off with Ash's hat. Ash can't find Aipom anywhere, but Team Rocket can — and does. Aipom jumped from a cliff onto a wobbly rock. Fortunately, Jesse is so in love with the adorable Normal-type that she risks life and limb to save it.

TRAVEL TIP
A great way to get to know a place is by tasting its unique foods. Festivals are perfect for sampling the local flavor!

When Ash finally catches up with Aipom, he can't believe Jesse rescued it and agrees to let her borrow the Pokémon for the contest. Aipom is super-psyched to enter and show off with Jesse, which makes Ash jealous.

At the contest, Dawn and Pachirisu put on a stunning show, although Pachirisu gets nervous and accidentally zaps the audience. However, the real Round-One showstopper is Aipom's Swift. Both Jesse and Dawn move onto Round Two, but Aipom easily beats Pachirisu, giving Jesse her first contest win! The prize is a year's supply of bananas, which Team Rocket happily carts off in their hot-air balloon.

Much to everyone's surprise, Aipom jumps on their balloon as it takes off, which breaks Ash's heart. But Aipom jumps straight back into Ash's arms after it snags a few bananas. Turns out Aipom just wanted some free fruit. Happy to be back with Ash, it runs off with his hat again. What a jokester!

AIPOM
Type: Normal Height: 2' 07"
Weight: 25.4 lbs
Normal-type Aipom may act as goofy as clowns, but their tails can pack a serious punch.

Pokémon: Diamond and Pearl, Episode 23
Faced With Steelix Determination

While Jesse, James, and Meowth are shoveling for treasure in the woods, they strike a Steelix. Their shovels get stuck in its head, so it bursts through the ground to chase them.

Just down the road, Brock is tending to a wounded Bidoof when the crew sees the angry Steelix storming their way. Bidoof leads them through a slit in the mountain to safety. Meowth follows them to a magnificent waterfall where a colony of timid Bidoof live.

TRAVEL TIP

Just off the path to Floaroma Town, there is a tall waterfall in the mountain range that a bunch of Bidoof like to call home.

After the Steelix blasts them off, James and Jesse are dropped back with Meowth. But the reunion is bittersweet because the powerful Pokémon is trying to bust its way through the slit in the mountain. Ash leads the effort to block the slit by hauling rocks with Brock. Meanwhile, the Bidoof create a dam by gnawing down trees and stacking them up. While Piplup distracts the Steelix with BubbleBeam, Dawn comes up with a solution to get the shovels out of its head and calm it down.

In an uncharacteristically bold move, the Bidoof bravely decide to jump on top of Steelix to pry the shovels loose. Their plan works! After they've relieved Steelix's painful headache, it peacefully returns to the forest.

STEELIX

Type: Steel/Ground

Height: 30' 02"

Weight: 881.8 lbs

Solid as a rock, the gigantic Steel-and-Ground-type has the hardest body of any Pokémon. While Steelix prefer to live underground, near mountains, or in caves, their snaky silver bodies shine in the light.

ON THE ROAD

Pokémon: Diamond and Pearl, Episode 24
Cooking Up a Sweet Story!

Teresa, a girl who runs a bake shop with her aunt, spots Pikachu's impressive Thunderbolt and introduces herself to the crew. She tells them about her Aunt Abigail, whose best friend and baking partner is a Pikachu she nicknamed Sugar. It has been missing for a few days and a big bake-off competition is coming up, so Teresa asks Ash if she can borrow Pikachu.

Pikachu goes to help Aunt Abigail collect Aspear Berries for her special cake recipe, and Team Rocket spots Pikachu zapping the fruit in the woods. Aunt Abigail uses strategy to fend off Seviper and blast Team Rocket off in two smooth moves. Ash is grateful to her, but the guilt of lying about Pikachu's identity is starting to take its toll on him.

When Ash goes to fess up, Abigail already seems to know about the switcheroo. She also confesses her own guilt over Sugar's disappearance. She tells him when Sugar wasn't able to crack open the Aspear Berries with its Thunderbolt, Abigail put pressure on it to perform, which she believes made it run away.

But they both have bigger problems now that Team Rocket has rolled up in an Aspear Berry robo-tank and grabbed Pikachu. Staravia and Ash try to stop them, but all of a sudden a massive Thunderbolt cuts open the tank. It's Sugar! And it's evolved into Raichu.

After it rescues Pikachu, Raichu blasts Team Rocket off and returns to Abigail. Auntie and her Sugar are happy to be reunited, but Ash, Brock, Dawn, Teresa, and Pikachu are even happier to chow down on Abigail's award-winning cake!

TRAVEL TIP

Wild Aspear Berries are delicious to eat, but hard as rocks. So be sure to look out for the falling fruit when passing through the woods!

RAICHU

Type: Electric Height: 2' 07"

Weight: 66.1 lbs

The evolved form of Pikachu, this Electric-type Pokémon can shock and amaze you with its 100,000-volt Thunderbolt.

FLOAROMA TOWN

A Pokémon paradise with flower power!

The cream of the crop, Floaroma Town is filled with sweet-smelling flowers and friendly people.

FLOAROMA TOWN

Pokémon: Diamond and Pearl, Episode 25
Oh Do You Know the Poffin Plan!

After arriving in Floaroma Town, Dawn, Ash, Brock and Pikachu arrive at a blossoming berry garden for a special Pokémon cooking lesson. Forsythia, who tends to the garden, is their instructor, but her shy Pokémon, Roserade, is afraid of strangers and hides from them. While Ash burns his batch, the Pokémon can't seem to get enough of Brock's poffins.

When Meowth eats one of Dawn's poffin treats out of the trash, he finds it so delicious that Team Rocket tries to steal all the berries in their giant robo-basket. Pikachu, Piplup, and Turtwig attempt to fend of Team Rocket, Carnivine, Dustox, and Cacnea, but it's no use against the robo-basket.

All of a sudden, help arrives. It's Roserade wrapped in a red scarf Forsythia gave it when it was just a little bitty Budew. In its disguise, Roserade is brave and strong like a superhero, and it even wows Forsythia with its ability to fight back.

However, while Mime Jr. distracts it with Tickle, Meowth grabs the scarf and Team Rocket nabs Roserade. As they roll off with their basket full of berries and Roserade, Forsythia stands in the middle of the road to block Team Rocket all by herself. She calls on Roserade to attack and reminds it that its strength doesn't come from a scarf, but from within.

Together with Piplup, Pikachu, and Croagunk, Roserade rips through the robo-basket and blasts Team Rocket off. To celebrate, Roserade releases Sunny Day, and amazingly, it regrows the entire field of berries. Dawn plucks a few to try out her new poffin recipe, and they're delicious!

TRAVEL TIP

Floaroma Town was once a barren wasteland. Until one day, legend has it, a young lady climbed a mountain to give thanks for nature's great beauty. Overnight it blossomed into the beautiful garden it is today.

ROSERADE

Type: Grass/Poison

Height: 2' 11" Weight: 32 lbs

Roserade, the evolved form of Budew, looks and smells sweet as a flower, but its attacks can be pretty nasty. The graceful Grass-and-Poison-type twirls like a ballerina to sting with its sharp thorns.

FLOAROMA TOWN

Pokémon: Diamond and Pearl, Episode 26
Getting the Pre-Contest Jitters!

A new Trainer who already knows Dee Dee, er Dawn, shows up. It's Kenny, Dawn's friend from preschool, who insists on calling her by her babyish nickname. He is in town to compete in the Floaroma Contest with his Prinplup, the evolved form of Piplup. When Piplup goes to introduce itself, Prinplup gives it a smack.

TRAVEL TIP
Floaroma Town is known for its gorgeous gardens, which make the fresh air smell like lovely perfume. It's natural aromatherapy!

Kenny upsets Dawn with his stories, which range from his experiences as a Trainer at the Grand Festival, where he lost to Zoey, to baby Dawn cutting her own hair like a Chimchar. While Kenny challenges Ash to a battle, he refuses to fight Dawn because he says she's not good enough. Dawn gets mad, but James and Meowth disturb everyone when they use Seviper to try to steal Prinplup.

As they're sneaking off, Piplup surprises everyone with a new move: Whirlpool. It sends Prinplup power and gives the Pokémon the strength to break free from Seviper. Together Piplup and its new buddy, Prinplup, blast Team Rocket off. And not a moment too soon — the Floaroma Pokémon Contest is starting!

Dawn is up first with Pachirisu, but after an awesome showing of Spotlight, the Pokémon accidentally slides into the judges' stand. Can Dawn recover from the slip up?

PRINPLUP
Type: Water Height: 2' 07"
Weight: 50.7 lbs
The Water-type that evolves from a cute little Piplup grows to be twice the size and almost five times as heavy. This blue bird has powerful wings that can snap a tree like a twig!

FLOAROMA TOWN

Pokémon: Diamond and Pearl, Episode 27
Settling a Not-So-Old Score!

It's the first round of the Floaroma contest. Dawn is on, but Pachirisu is off — literally! The Electric-type is suffering from stage fright. Dawn tosses a poffin treat in the air. Pachirisu quickly jumps up to eat it. Now they're back on track and strutting their stuff!

Jesse has also entered the contest in her Trainer disguise, Jesselina. She shows off Seviper. Then it's Kenny's turn. He amazes the audience with Alakazam.

Backstage, Dawn is worried her rough start with Pachirisu will stop the judges from selecting her as a top contender. Lo and behold, Kenny, Jesselina, and Dawn all make it to Round Two!

Dawn is delighted but focused, and she and Piplup win the battle against Jesselina and Dustox. Now she has to fight her childhood friend, Kenny. It's Piplup versus its evolved form, Prinplup. Based on size and strength, the winner seems obvious, but Piplup uses its new move, Whirlpool, to win!

Dawn proudly accepts her first contest award, the fabulous Floaroma Ribbon.

TRAVEL TIP

MC Marion hosts all the Pokémon Contests in the Sinnoh Region. Since she travels around so much, she's a good resource for Trainers who want to get the lay of the land.

ALAKAZAM

Type: Psychic Height: 4' 11"

Weight: 105.8 lbs

Alakazam is so smart its super brain has more memory than a computer hard drive. An evolved form of Abra, this Psychic-type Pokémon's IQ is off the charts.

Pokémon: Diamond and Pearl, Episode 28
Drifloon in the Wind

Dawn, Ash, and Brock decide to stop at a Pokémon Center, where they are greeted by Nurse Joy's daughters, Paige and Marnie. While Marnie is carried off by some Drifloon to bring her dad lunch, Paige takes Ash to feed wild Pokémon. She leads him to a secret river where a Legendary Suicune lives.

Marnie arrives at the Valley Wind Works Power Plant and delivers lunch, but Team Rocket is already there. They try to steal Ampharos, but it uses an Electric-type attack to blast them off. Unfortunately, the attack was so strong, it destroys the power plant's wiring and the town blacks out.

TRAVEL TIP
The local Pokémon Center has a team of Drifloon that can airlift patients and even people.

Back at the Pokémon Center, Nurse Joy is nervous about her husband and leaves to see if he needs any help. A storm is brewing, and Pikachu tries to stop Paige from following her mom, but they both get carried away on a Drifloon. Ash, Brock, Dawn, and Marnie run after Paige, but when they arrive at the power plant, she's not there.

Ash flies on a Drifloon to locate them while Joy and the crew hop in a van. A boulder has been knocked into the road so they don't make it very far. Marnie heads out on foot through the lightning and pouring rain to call on Suicune for help. Meanwhile, the wind knocks Ash and Drifloon down, but luckily he finds Paige.

When it stops raining, Ash leads Paige to a log bridge. When they're just a step away from safety, the wood snaps, and Paige and Ash are in a free fall!

Just in time, Suicune swoops in and saves them! But before the crew can thank Suicune, the magical Pokémon disappears.

Pokémon: Diamond and Pearl, Episode 29 The Champ Twins!

Ash, Brock, Dawn, and Pikachu are on their way to Eterna City when a reporter named Rhonda approaches them. She's covering battles for her show, *Sinnoh Now*, and she's looking for Trainers to challenge the unbeatable Champ Twins.

Ash introduces himself to the brothers, Brian and Ryan. They tell Ash they're up for a battle, but they only play tag team. Dawn and Piplup volunteer to join Ash, so they hit the field. It's the Champ Twins with Croconaw and Quilava vs. Dawn and Ash with Piplup and Turtwig.

Despite their enthusiasm, Ash and Dawn can't seem to outdo Ryan and Brian. After their defeat, Dawn and Ash start fighting, and so do Piplup and Turtwig. Pikachu breaks them up with a Thunderbolt, but it's clear teamwork is their main issue.

Ash and Dawn talk things over and decide to take on the Champ Twins again, as a real team this time. When they return to the field, Ryan and Brian have fallen into one of Team Rocket's traps, and are being taken away in their hot-air balloon. Quickly, Ash sends Staravia to slit the balloon. It crash-lands, and the fighting really begins! Team Rocket, Seviper, and Carnivine try to crush Piplup and Turtwig, but Ash and Dawn are united. They rescue the stolen Pokémon and blast off the troublesome trio.

The grateful Champ Twins agree to battle Dawn and Ash again. Working together, Dawn and Ash are unstoppable match. They cream the Champ Twins.

Victory is sweet, but cooperation makes everyone a winner!

TRAVEL TIP

If you're up for the test, you can challenge the Champ Twins to a tag-team battle at their camp in the Eterna Forest.

Pokémon: Diamond and Pearl, Episode 30

Some Enchanted Sweetening!

While the crew is wandering through Eterna Forest, Cheryl the Treasure Hunter arrives with Chansey, who instantly attracts an adorable Burmy. They soon catch the male Burmy, which Cheryl adds to her three evolved female Burmy Wormadam.

Ash, Dawn, and Brock are impressed by Cheryl's collection. She tells them about her quest to find the Enchanted Honey, which is hidden at the mythical Amber Castle. Only an evolved male Burmy, Mothim, can lead her to the honey treasure. But Team Rocket overhears her plans, and they decide to beat her to the golden honey.

TRAVEL TIP

In the Eterna Forest, there are Combee that create sweet-smelling honey that attracts Pokémon.

Since Burmy has to win a battle to evolve, Ash offers a battle with Turtwig. Turtwig easily defeats the Burmy, so Ash proposes a round with Pikachu. While Pikachu falls over after one attack from Burmy, Team Rocket grabs the Bug-type Pokémon from their hot-air balloon!

Team Rocket sneaks away under cover of Seviper's smoke screen. Jesse and James feed Burmy so it's strong enough to fight, but it still loses to Meowth. Before Wobbuffet has a chance to battle it, Staravia helps the crew locate Team Rocket.

Together, Turtwig, Piplup, Pikachu, and Burmy blast Team Rocket off! At its first taste of victory, Burmy evolves into a magnificent flying Mothim. From the sky, it leads Cheryl, Ash, Dawn, Brock and Pikachu toward the Amber Castle.

BURMY

Type: Bug Height: 0' 08"

Weight: 7.5 lbs

Burmy, a Bug-type Pokémon, comes wrapped in different cloaks depending on where it has battled. Even after it evolves from winning a fight — females into Wormadam and males into Mothim — it still retains the looks of its original location.

Burmy (Sandy Cloak)

Burmy (Trash Cloak)

Burmy (Grass Cloak)

Pokémon: Diamond and Pearl, Episode 3I
The Grass-type Is Always Greener

On their quest to find the Amber Castle, Mothim leads Cheryl, Ash, Brock, Dawn, and Pikachu to a green patch, where they find a new friend — Gardenia. She is a Grass-type Pokémon fanatic, but little do they know, she's also the Eterna City Gym Leader! So when Gardenia offers to battle Ash, he has no idea what an opportunity it truly is.

TRAVEL TIP
Combee make the Enchanted Honey from the nectar of the pomeg flower.

While Gardenia and Cherubi can't beat Ash and his tough Turtwig, Gardenia's Turtwig alone is able to beat both Staravia and Ash's Turtwig. Gardenia sure has a way with Grass-types!

That night, Cheryl tells Gardenia all about her quest for the Enchanted Honey. Gardenia tells her about a wall in the forest where a colony of Combee live.

Before they can head out, Team Rocket blocks the road. Gardenia tries to make a trade with James for his Carnivine. The crew tries to warn her, but Jesse and James have already begun their attack. From their hot-air balloon, Team Rocket swipes Mothim. Gardenia and Turtwig destroy the balloon's robot arm and Pikachu blasts them off with a zap!

As they approach a garden of Pomeg flowers, a messenger Nuzleaf calls Gardenia away to another emergency. Mothim is too excited to leave and hovers over the garden. A Combee flies out of a flower, and the crew chases it. They must be getting close to the Amber Castle!

COMBEE

Type: Bug/Flying Height: I' 00"
Weight: I2.I lbs

This Bug-and-Flying-type Pokémon is a self-contained comb with two wings, two antennae, and three faces. While some might say that three's company, Combee love to stack up and sleep in a crowded hive.

THE WALL OF COMBEE & THE AMBER CASTLE

Pokémon: Diamond and Pearl, Episode 32 The Angry Combeenation!

When Mothim leads them to a waterfall with thousands of Combee, the crew is sure they're near the Amber Castle! Pikachu picks up the sweet scent of honey and leads Ash, Brock, Dawn, and Cheryl behind the falls and into a dark cave.

Team Rocket is following their trail — but they're not fast enough. Once they get behind the water, they can't see the crew in the dark cave, so they just start digging for the honey treasure.

Meanwhile, Mothim leads Ash, Dawn, Brock, and Cheryl though a crack in the cave to a rock crystal corridor that sparkles with light. A mob of angry Combee swarm them, and as they run back through the cave, they encounter Team Rocket. While Jesse and James take out Seviper and Cacnea to battle, Ash tries to make peace, explaining that they are just there to find the Amber Castle. Cheryl doesn't want to fight, so she asks Mothim to use Supersonic to confuse all the Pokémon. Dawn calls on Piplup to wash Team Rocket clean out of there!

TRAVEL TIP

In the dark cave, there's a light at the end of the tunnel! Before the Amber Castle is a bright beacon — a crystal corridor.

Now they're back on track as Mothim leads them through the cave and past a giant Wall of Combee. There lies the amazing Amber Castle, its giant cups overflowing with Enchanted Honey, along with hundreds of Combee guards and their regal leader, Vespiquen. Cheryl bravely approaches the throne, tells the story of her hunt, and humbly asks for a cup full of honey.

Just then, Team Rocket bursts in, unleashes Seviper and Cacnea, and starts stealing buckets of the precious honey. When the Combee try to fight back, the palace begins to crack. While the crew scrambles to stop the palace from crumbling, Pachirisu uses Sweet Kiss to stop Seviper and Cacnea. Vespiquen blasts Team Rocket off, covering them in the sticky stuff they tried to steal. The Combee quickly go to work repairing the cracks by filling them with Enchanted Honey.

Vespiquen, grateful for all the help fending off Team Rocket, fulfills Cheryl's mission and hands her a golden cup full of honey. Cheryl shares the honey with all her new pals, but it is a bittersweet good-bye. Cheryl must continue on hunting for treasure, and Ash has to get to Eterna City to try to win another gym badge!

VESPIQUEN

Type: Bug/Flying
Height: 3' 11"
Weight: 84.9 lbs

Royal Vespiquen is truly the queen of her Combee hive. A dynamic diva, the Bug-and-Flying-type can only evolve from a female and keeps Combee babies safe in her skirt.

ON THE ROAD

Pokémon: Diamond and Pearl, Episode 33
All Dressed Up With Somewhere to Go!

Up the road, Rhonda the reporter is hosting a televised Pokémon Dress-Up Contest! The grand prize is a precious Pokémon Egg.

Dawn puts Piplup in a Weedle outfit, but when it busts out BubbleBeam, they get disqualified. Brock enters Croagunk, who is committed to his Politoed costume and acts the part. Ash enters Pikachu, who uses physical comedy to morph into a bunch of its Pokémon pals. Jesse, disguised as a cowgirl, enters Meowth as Weevil and Jameson, aka James, enters Mime Jr.

TRAVEL TIP
If you hear a chopper race through the sky in Sinnoh, it's probably Rhonda the reporter and her film crew chasing a story in their helicopter.

However, when it's time for the second round, Team Rocket steals the prize and makes a break for it. Officer Jenny and her Growlithe go after them, but Team Rocket flies away in their hot-air balloon.

Ash sends Staravia after them and Piplup uses BubbleBeam, but Jesse and James can't stop fighting over who would have won the contest. Soon no one is able to pilot the balloon. The Pokémon Egg ends up falling over the edge.

Dawn sends Buneary catch it. Then Pikachu blasts Team Rocket off with Thunderbolt.

Thanks to the crew's efforts, the Egg is awarded to the most deserving Pokémon Dress-Up Contest Winner — Brock!

Pokémon: Diamond and Pearl, Episode 34
Buizel Your Way Out of This!

On their way to Eterna City, Ash, Dawn, and Brock pass a fisherman carrying his exhausted Zigzagoon. He warns them about an unbeatable Buizel at the river, but that only makes the crew want to battle the Pokémon!

TRAVEL TIP
Be sure to bring your tackle box and fishing pole, because there are some real catches down at the river!

The crew sets up fishing rods to lure the Buizel, but Zoey catches them first. What a nice surprise! Zoey is at the river looking to catch a Water-type Pokémon.

All of a sudden, the infamous Buizel is hooked on Dawn's rod! Piplup swings into action, but is easily defeated by the strong swimmer. Buizel then challenges Zoey with Glameow, and then Ash with Pikachu, but no one can beat it in battle.

Ash is now even more determined to catch it, so he starts training with Pikachu. But Team Rocket barges in and nabs Buizel with a net. Piplup and Pikachu strike Seviper and Carnivine. Now free, Buizel blasts them off.

Buizel still wants to battle, so it challenges Piplup again. At first, Dawn can't catch it with her Poké Ball, but with Piplup's Whirlpool and BubbleBeam combination, she has finally secured a new friend.

After an exciting day, the crew heads back out on the road to Eterna City.

BUIZEL
Type: Water
Height: 2' 04" Weight: 65.0 lbs
Buizel is a playful Water-type Pokémon that likes to splash around. A strong swimmer, it has an innertube at its neck to help it float.

Pokémon: Diamond and Pearl, Episode 35
An Elite Meet and Greet!

The crew's new pal Buizel keeps picking fights with everyone. It won't listen to Dawn, it won't practice with Piplup, and it takes things too far when it battles Turtwig. Brock, Ash, and Dawn bring Turtwig to rest at the Pokémon Center, but Dawn doesn't know how to repair her relationship with Buizel.

While they're waiting in the lobby, Lucian, a Psychic-type Pokémon Trainer and member of the Sinnoh Region's Elite Four, strolls in. The crew is respectful — all except Buizel, who immediately challenges him to a battle. Lucian and Bronzong win a swift victory, and Buizel is really defeated.

TRAVEL TIP
The top Trainers are known as the Elite Four. In order to battle the Pokémon specialists in this region, you have to win the Sinnoh League.

While Buizel is outside of the Pokémon Center, Team Rocket catches it and sails away in their hot-air balloon. Lucian stops Ash, Brock, and Dawn from helping because he thinks Buizel can rescue itself and that will help it feel strong again.

Just as Lucian predicted, Buizel bursts free and is ready to take on Team Rocket, Carnivine, and Seviper. Lucian instructs Buizel and for once, it actually listens!

After it blasts Team Rocket off, Buizel asks to battle Lucian and Bronzong again. This time, Buizel listens to Dawn. Although Dawn and Buizel are finally working as a team, Lucian cuts off the battle and congratulates Dawn and Buizel on their progress. As he walks off into the sunset, he tells Dawn he looks forward to battling her again.

BRONZONG

Type: Steel/Psychic

Height: 4' 03" Weight: 412.3 lbs

Bronzong was uncovered after being buried for two thousand years at a construction site. It is so in tune with nature that it's regarded as the Pokémon that brings plentiful harvests because it has the power to make rain.

ETERNA CITY

Where the grass is always greener!

While the fresh grass that covers this historic city will make you want to walk around barefoot, it's the impressive collection at the local museum that will knock your socks off.

ETERNA CITY MUSEUM

Pokémon: Diamond and Pearl, Episode 36
The Secret Sphere of Influence

During a visit to the museum in Eterna City, the Adamant Orb, a diamond the size of a soccer ball, is stolen from the collection. The security tape reveals the thief to be a Sunflora, but under that Grass-type disguise is Meowth!

The museum is surrounded by guards and helicopters. Two Officer Jenny's team up, and Gardenia is called in to help the hunt, too. Nando and his Sunflora were visiting the museum when the heist occurred, so Nando is immediately arrested. Ash, Dawn, and Brock offer to help find the real culprits.

While the thieving Team Rocket hides in a storage closet to prepare their escape, Piplup and Sunflora spy on them through the air duct. Jesse and James put on suits to disguise themselves as business people, and James hides the orb under his jacket like it's his belly.

TRAVEL TIP

The Adamant Orb is a big, beautiful diamond. Its true value lies in its flash, which can magnify the power of Dialga, the Legendary Pokémon of Time.

As Piplup pecks through the duct to pick a fight with Team Rock, Ash, Dawn and Brock rush over to help — but they are confused because all they see is a couple of business people. Sunflora quickly slashes open their disguises.

But Team Rocket still won't give up the priceless orb, that is, unless, they get paid off. So, Officer Jenny asks Stunky to squirt its gnarly smell, which makes Jesse drop the orb so she can cover her nose.

Team Rocket makes a break for it, and the guards let them go by since they smell so awful. However, worse than the stink is scheming Team Galactic, the brains behind the heist.

All's well that ends well, and Nando's good name is cleared. He graciously thanks his friends for their help with a song!

STUNKY

Type: Poison/Dark

Height: I' 04" **Weight:** 42.3 lbs

If you smell something funky, it just might be because of a Stunky. The Poison-and-Dark-type Pokémon packs a putrid punch that lasts for twenty-four hours.

Pokémon: Diamond and Pearl, Episode 37
A Grass Menagerie

Gardenia greets Ash, Brock, Dawn, and Pikachu at her garden paradise — the Eterna City Gym. Ash immediately challenges her to a rematch, so Cherubi and Turtwig begin the battle. Although Ash's Turtwig was able to defeat Cherubi back in the woods, it has to get taken out of this fight early. Staravia steps in and defeats Cherubi, but it isn't able to beat Gardenia and Turtwig. So Ash brings Turtwig back to battle to make it an even match.

This time, when Gardenia and Turtwig whip out Leech Seed, it doesn't keep Ash and Turtwig down for the count. They are victorious! Gardenia and Roserade try to take on Turtwig, so Ash brings Aipom in for reinforcement. Although it is blinded by Roserade's powerful attacks, it relies on its sense of sound and Ash acts as its eyes. Together, Ash wins his second gym battle in Sinnoh — and the Forest Badge!

Meanwhile Team Rocket has been mining jewels for an Eterna City Underground Explorer. So although Ash has cause to celebrate, trouble lies just below the surface.

TRAVEL TIP

The Eterna City Gym is a Grass-type Pokémon's playground. It so lush and green — full of all their favorite things!

CHERUBI

Type: Grass

Height: I' 04" **Weight:** 7.3 lbs.

Two heads are better than one — and Cherubi, a Grass-type, is perfect proof. The round, pink Pokémon has an extra-small face that is full of nutrients.

Pokémon: Diamond and Pearl, Episode 38
One Big Happiny Family

The Egg Brock won at the Pokémon Dress-Up Contest looks like it's about to hatch! So Ash, Dawn, Brock, and Pikachu pull over at a nearby Pokémon Center, but the place looks abandoned.

Chansey points them toward Nurse Joy, who is off in the woods. Brock tells her that he needs her help, since there's a Pokémon ready to pop out! Nurse Joy snaps into action, and a Happiny is hatched.

Brock is one proud papa as he introduces Happiny around, gives her a bath, and smoothes a white stone for her pouch. But while she's playing with Pikachu, Team Rocket's claw catches Happiny and they sail away in their hot air balloon. Jesse is planning to evolve Happiny into Chansey so she can start her own chain of Pokémon Centers where she can steal from even more unsuspecting Trainers.

Despite Team Rocket's silly faces, nothing can seem to cheer up the captured baby Happiny — that is, until Brock shows up to rescue it. Sudowoodo tries to stop Cacnea, but Happiny surprises everyone with its strength as it chucks Seviper and saves the day! Brock goes to pick up Happiny to give it a hug, but the Normal-type Pokémon actually lifts him up and gives him a big hug!

Together, the crew heads for Hearthome City with their new family member, Happiny!

TRAVEL TIP

If you're headed toward Hearthome City and have a need for speed, you can ride into town on the new bicycle highway.

HAPPINY

Type: Normal Height: 2' 00"

Weight: 53.8 lbs

Happiny is an adorable round Normal-type that's fun to have around. The playful pink Pokémon loves to keep a stone in its pouch, but if it really loves you, Happiny will give the stone to you — along with her heart.

Pokémon: Diamond and Pearl, Episode 39
Steamboat Willies

The crew spots a steamboat and decides to hop on for some sightseeing. Ash, Brock, and Dawn head to town to pick up some snacks while Piplup and Pikachu agree to baby-sit their Pokémon pals.

All the Pokémon are having fun in the sun, but Pachirisu keeps causing trouble. Its Electric-type Attack powers on the controls of the ship, and it accidentally steers the ship into the ocean!

Meanwhile, Team Rocket has jumped on board and is pretending to be exercise instructors. The crew quickly realizes the exercise instructors are imposters and blast them off.

When Ash, Brock, and Dawn return, they wake up the captain. He offers them a ride on Mantyke to rescue the ship. Ash and Dawn signal Pikachu and Piplup that they're here to help. Piplup tries to turn the ship around with Whirlpool, and Buneary uses Ice Beam, but nothing seems to work. The boat is headed straight for a giant rock!

Buizel comes to the rescue and breaks the rock up. One of the stone scraps is headed for the ship, and Mantyke quickly maneuvers to destroy it before it can hit the boat.

The crew decides they've had enough of a water adventure, so they continue on to Hearthome City on dry land.

TRAVEL TIP

Taking a steamboat tour is a great way to see the Sinnoh Region. You can catch up with a cruise ship just outside of Hearthome City.

MANTYKE

Type: Water/Flying
Height: 3' 03"
Weight: 143.3 lbs

This Water-and-Flying-type Pokémon soars through the sea and sky. If you look at the markings on its back, you can tell which region each Mantyke is from.

Pokémon: Diamond and Pearl, Episode 40
Top-Down Training!

When the crew spots Cynthia, the Pokémon League Champion of Sinnoh, at the shrine to the Legendary Ancient Pokémon Dialga and Palkia, they are starstruck! But before they can get a word in, Paul has challenged her to a six-Pokémon battle.

A crowd gathers to watch as Cynthia and Garchomp crush Paul, Chimchar, Weavile, Murkrow, and Torterra. With the crowd heckling him, Paul calls the battle off early. Despite all the cruel things Paul has said to him, Ash defends him. But Paul's ego can't handle defeat. He starts to storm off — until Cynthia steps in and makes him take his Pokémon to get a check-up with Nurse Joy.

When they arrive at the Pokémon Center, Nurse Joy is busy with surgery, so Cynthia treats the Pokémon herself. Then she leads the crew back to the stone shrine, where she tells them about her quest to find the truth behind the origins of the Pokémon world.

Meanwhile, Team Rocket steals Chimchar. As they fire up their hot-air balloon, Chimchar chars them. Paul calls on Ursaring to blast them off.

Meanwhile, a news report informs the crew that a lustrous orb related to Palkia, the Legendary Pokémon of Space, was just uncovered in Celestic Town. Everyone decides to follow their dreams — Cynthia will travel to the ancient Pokémon discovery, while the crew continues on to Hearthome City to compete!

TRAVEL TIP

The ancient stone shrine with carvings about the Legendary Pokémon Dialga and Palkia is one of the few sources of information on the mysterious origins of Pokémon.

GARCHOMP

Type: Dragon/Ground

Height: 6' 03" Weight: 209.4 lbs

The Dragon-and-Ground-type Garchomp can fly fast to take a bite out of its opponents in battle.

Pokémon: Diamond and Pearl, Episode 4I
Stand Up Sit Down

While Pikachu and Piplup are playing in the woods, Misdreavus and Glameow come and ask them for help. Brock, Ash, and Dawn follow them and find Zoey, who has injured her foot. Brock uses his first-aid kit to help her heal, and they take her back to her campsite. There, Zoey introduces them to sweet Shellos, a pink Pokémon she just befriended in the river.

TRAVEL TIP
Keep an eye out for Brock! A skilled medic, Brock can heal almost any Pokémon or human injury with his travel first-aid kit.

Together with Glameow and Shellos, Zoey puts on quite a show with a double move she plans on using at the Pokémon Contest in Hearthome City. Dawn had no idea that the contest was a doubles competition. When she tries to practice moves with Piplup and Pachirisu, she winds up shocked by an Electric-type.

Just as her friends make Dawn feel better, Jesse shows up in her Jesselina disguise. She makes fun of Dawn and challenges Zoey to a rematch — a battle off the contest stage. Along with Glameow and Shellos, Zoey defeats Jesselina, Seviper, and Dustox. Dawn is even more inspired by Zoey, who despite her injury is still a strong competitor, and looks forward to seeing her again in Hearthome City!

SHELLOS (EAST SEA)

SHELLOS
Type: Water
Height: I' 00" Weight: I3.9 lbs
Shellos, a Water-type Pokémon, loves to live by the seashore. You can tell which coast it came from by its coloring — pink for west, blue for east.

SHELLOS (WEST SEA)

Pokémon: Diamond and Pearl, Episode 42
The Electrike Company

While Ash, Brock, Dawn, and all the Pokémon are playing in a river valley, an Electrike's blast bursts in. Jaco, a pony-tailed Pokémon breeder, runs up and apologizes for Electrike's attack gone awry. He introduces the crew to Cal, the head of the Pokémon Training Center for Electric-types.

TRAVEL TIP
If you have an Electric-type, you have to check out the fun facilities at the local Pokémon Training Center. It's right in the river valley, so it's perfect for relaxing and recharging.

Cal shows them around the facility, but it's empty since all the Pokémon graduated — except for this last Electrike that just can't seem to control its moves. Jaco blames himself for the poor training since he is a Flying-type expert. So Brock offers to teach him a few pointers and his secret Pokémon Food recipes. While they're cooking up a storm in the kitchen, Pikachu helps Electrike learn Thunderbolt.

James and Meowth are moved by the Pokémon's friendship. But despite their pleas, Jesse shoots a missile straight at Pikachu and Electrike. When Ash, Dawn, Brock, and Jaco come to check out the crash site, they are surprised to find James and Meowth protecting the Pokémon. Feeling betrayed, Jesse runs off into the woods alone.

The next morning, Jaco proudly prepares the Pokémon food, and Electrike hits the target in practice! Now it's time for the true field test, so Ash, James, and Meowth put on rubber jackets and become running targets.

As they begin the chase, Jesse rolls up in a robot and snatches Electrike. It gets so mad, it evolves into Manectric and busts out of her robot claws. But Jesse manages to win her friends back. James and Meowth decide to jump on board, and Pikachu blasts them off for good.

Impressed with Manectric's new skills, Cal finally graduates Electrike with honors!

Pokémon: Diamond and Pearl, Episode 43
Malice in Wonderland

Ash, Brock, Dawn, and Pikachu are looking for a Pokémon Center to spend the night. When it starts to rain, they seek shelter in an abandoned shack. When they realize it's not raining on the other side, the crew continues out the back gate. After a flash of light, they spot a colorful Pokémon Center.

Before Brock can compliment Nurse Joy, she tells him how much she likes him. Then Officer Jenny shows up and says the same thing! While Brock links arms with the ladies, Professor Oak and Johanna, Dawn's mom, challenge Ash and Dawn to battle to be the best!

TRAVEL TIP

While wandering in the woods, stay out of abandoned shacks — they could be the gate that leads you into one of Mismagius' illusions.

Ash and Dawn find themselves in the giant coliseum in front of thousands of cheering fans. In the stands, Brock is smiling because he's surrounded by Jennys and Joys, but they turn into Croagunk and Poison Jab him!

Brock wakes up from the dream-turned-nightmare to realize they all fell asleep in the woods after being hypnotized by Mismagius. The magical Pokémon shines a light, and Brock is back in dreamland again. But this time, he knows it's fake and he has to save his friends.

Meanwhile, Ash and Dawn have both won their battles and been awarded all the ribbons and badges from all the regions. Brock bursts their bubble and tells them all it's just a dream. Suddenly, they're stuck in a crumbling coliseum where they have to battle Mismagius, who has merged with Rayquaza. It chases them back to the shack, where the crew gets back to reality by crossing through the gate again.

On the other side, it's morning. The crew decides to continueon to Hearthome City!

MISMAGIUS

Type: Ghost

Height: 2' 11" Weight: 9.7 lbs

Beware of this mischievous Ghost-type. It bewitches with its hum and can cause dreamlike hallucinations.

Pokémon: Diamond and Pearl, Episode 44
Mass Hip-Po-Sis

While packing up to hit the road, Ash, Dawn, and Brock realize they're missing one important thing — Turtwig! It's off trying to help a Hippopotas that's stuck up in a tree. With Pikachu's aid, Ash is able to talk the scared Hippopotas down. As they're about to leave, Rhonda the reporter appears on the scene. She's been filming a documentary on the wild Hippopotas that has been wandering through the woods without its herd. So, Ash, Dawn, and Brock decide to help the Hippopotas find its way back home.

TRAVEL TIP
Rhonda the reporter covers the entire Sinnoh Region, but she constantly has to duck for cover. Her crew's boom mic always manages to hit her on the head. So if you see her with her camera crew, be prepared to dodge equipment!

Just then, Team Rocket swoops into to steal the stray Pokémon. They get the sand-loving Hippopotas soaked with water, but Ash gets rid of them with Aipom's help. The crew decides to take tired Hippopotas to the nearest Pokémon Center to rest. Ash and Staravia even import sand into the Center just so their new friend will get well soon.

However, before they can return Hippopotas to its home, Team Rocket returns. Turtwig takes on Cacnea, and Pikachu blasts them all off. Then, with the help of its new friends, Ash, Brock, Dawn and Pikachu, Hippopotas finally arrives back where it belongs — with its herd.

HIPPOPOTAS
Type: Ground
Height: 2' 07" Weight: 109.1 lbs
This Ground-type Pokémon hates water so much that it sweats sand! Known for its powerful Yawn Attack, Hippopotas like to travel in a pack.

Pokémon: Diamond and Pearl, Episode 45
Ill-Will Hunting

While Ash, Dawn, Brock, and Pikachu are walking through the Sinnoh Nature Preserve, they stumble upon some wild Shieldon. But Hunter J spots them, too, and swoop in on her Salamence.

Luckily, Gary Oak, who protects the Pokémon in the preserve, shows up to help the crew fend off the Pokémon poacher. They decide to team up and take the rare Shieldon to Professor Rowan's lab for safekeeping. But tricky Hunter J tracks them down. When the crew passes through some steep cliffs, she sneaks up on them and snatches one of the Rock-and-Steel-type Pokémon.

Before Hunter J can sell the priceless Pokémon to a wealthy collector, Pikachu, Umbreon, and Electivire combine their attacks to blast through Hunter J's hideout. The stolen Shieldon is saved!

TRAVEL TIP

Make sure you don't wear all brown when you're passing through the nature preserve — Shieldon like to head-butt tree trunks, and you might get mistaken for one!

SHIELDON

Type: Rock/Steel Height: 1' 08"

Weight: 125.7 lbs

Millions of years ago, the ancient Shieldon in this area roamed freely in the forests. Scientists were able to bring back the prehistoric Pokémon by cloning a fossil. Known for their rock-solid faces, the Rock-and-Steel-type Pokémon like to head-butt.

STONE MAZE

Pokémon: Diamond and Pearl, Episode 46
A-Maze-ing Race

While Ash, Brock and Dawn are racing to the Pokémon Center to pick up a new application for Dawn's Pokétch, they run into Team Rocket in disguise. Jesse, James, and Meowth tell the crew that there's a secret shortcut through this cave.

Inside, a group of Graveler and Golem roll through on a rampage, separating everybody. When Ash reaches the exit, he sees Paul atop a stone maze. But when Paul brushes him off, Ash heads back to find his friends. Meanwhile, Brock, Aipom, Turtwig, and Staravia bump into Paul next, but he doesn't help them either.

Golem and Graveler are being chased by an enormous Onix. Ash instructs Buizel and Piplup to use their Water-type attacks to stop Onix. Staravia leads the crew to reunite, but a wall still separates Brock and Dawn from Ash. So Aipom, Turtwig, Croagunk, Buizel, Sudowoodo, Happiny, Buneary, and Piplup combine their attacks to break through the stone.

While they're busy busting bricks, Team Rocket seizes Staravia. Pikachu climbs the pyramid and uses Iron Tail to crack open the cage. Then it hitches a ride on Staravia to blast Team Rocket off with Thunderbolt.

Now that the crew is together again, they hightail it to the Pokémon Center. There, Dawn receives the animated Coin Toss application for her Pokétch. As the crew continues on their journey, they reach a fork in the road. To decide which way to go next, they use the latest technology to flip a coin.

TRAVEL TIP

Cross through the cave to find a secret stone maze. Although its twists and turns will keep you on your toes, the resident Onix will keep you moving!

STARAVIA

Type: Normal/Flying **Height:** 2' 00"

Weight: 34.2 lbs

The evolved form of Starly, this frequent flier is great at spotting things from mid-air. Staravia can be found mostly in the Sinnoh Region and is often in packs with other Flying-type Pokémon.

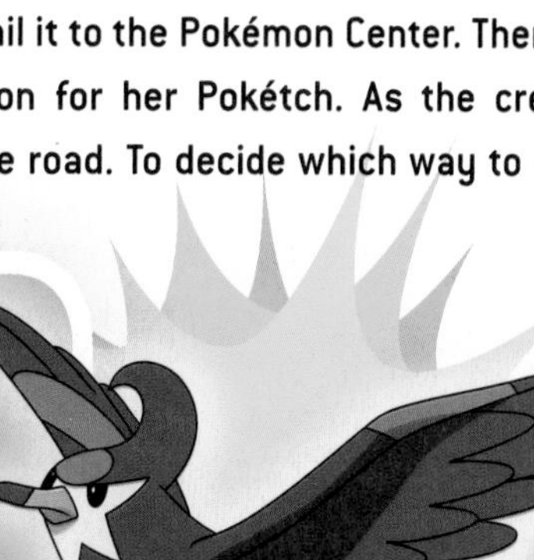

Pokémon: Diamond and Pearl, Episode 47
Sandshrew's Locker

Ash, Dawn, Brock and Pikachu meet Mira and Abra, who offer to teleport them to Hearthome City. The crew agrees — except instead of Hearthome City, Abra teleports them to the top of a dam. Then Mira asks them for a favor. Her grandmother's pin is buried at the bottom of the water, and she needs Buizel and Piplup's help to find it. Then she'll teleport them to Hearthome City.

TRAVEL TIP
If you like to dive, be sure to check out the river dam. At the bottom, there's an entire city covered in water and Water-type Pokémon. Just be careful you don't disturb the natural habitats or the Gyarados!

Although they don't like being tricked, Ash, Dawn, and Brock are always willing to help a friend in need. Mira leads them into an abandoned underwater city, where a Gyarados attacks. Brock asks Mira to explain why she keeps tricking them. She says she used to live in that underwater town and she accidentally left her first Pokémon there when they were evacuated. It is still sitting in its Poké Ball, waiting for her.

Touched by her story, the crew decides to give it another go. Together, Piplup, Buizel, and Pikachu stop Gyarados, and Mira recovers the Poké Ball.

After the battle, Team Rocket swims up and snatches Abra and Mira. Abra uses its teleport to transports them out of the net, and Pikachu blasts them off.

Mira is finally reunited with her special Sandshrew. As thanks for all their help, Mira and Abra teleport the whole crew to scenic Hearthome City!

ABRA
Type: Psychic Height: 2' 11" Weight: 43.0 lbs
Even while it's sleeping, Abra can teleport anywhere — to avoid danger or just to take a fun trip. No need to tell this Pokémon what you're thinking — it is also a mind reader.

HEARTHOME CITY

Home is where the heart is!

Warm, welcoming Hearthome City is the perfect place for traveling trainers to pair up and battle their Pokémon.

Pokémon: Diamond and Pearl, Episode 48
Dawn's Early Night

When Ash, Brock, Dawn, and Pikachu reach the Hearthome Gym, they are welcomed by the wandering bard Nando and Kricketune. Although Ash was ready to battle for another badge, he's bummed to find out the Hearthome Gym Leader is away on a journey. Nando tries to cheer him up by telling them about the Tag-Team Battle, the most famous competition in town. Brock and Ash decide to register for the two-Trainer battle! Nando and Dawn plan on entering the doubles Pokémon Hearthome Contest.

Backstage, Dawn rallies her Pokémon with a motivational speech, but she's secretly nervous. On stage, Nando kicks off the contest with Kricketune and Sunflora, who serenade the audience. Jesse, disguised as Jesselina, tickles herself and the audience with Mime Jr. and Cacnea. Zoey, Glameow, and Shellos are spectacular. Dawn, Piplup, and Pachirisu stun with a Sweet Kiss and BubbleBeam combo.

Although Dawn is confident she's going to win this contest, she doesn't get selected for the second round, even though her friends do. Nando and Zoey try to comfort her, but she runs off crying. Like a true champ, she shakes off her sadness and comes back in time to support her pals.

In the final round, Nando beats Zoey in battle and wins the Hearthome City Ribbon. Later than night, Zoey and Dawn talk about their disappointing days and promise to never let losing keep them down.

TRAVEL TIP

Hearthome City is for pairs, from its competitions to its contests. After all, two is always better than one!

KRICKETUNE

Type: Bug Height: 3' 03"

Weight: 56.2 lbs

The evolved form of Kricketot, Kricketune composes complex and cool melodies to express its feelings. This Bug-type makes beautiful music!

Pokémon: Diamond and Pearl, Episode 49
Tag! We're It!

Dawn is still crushed from her loss at the Hearthome City Pokémon Contest, so Ash, Brock, and Zoey register Dawn for the Tag-Team battle to build her confidence back up. Each contestant is given a number and then is randomly teamed up with another Trainer for the competition. Dawn get matched with a mathematical genius, Conway, and his Slowking. Brock may have met his mate with his partner Holly, who, in a bizarre twist of fate, has a crazy crush on him!

But things don't go so well for Ash, who becomes Paul's partner. Pikachu tries to make peace with Paul and Elekid, but it winds up getting zapped when it goes to shake hands. Then Chimchar nearly chars Ash in practice, but Paul complains he's only in the contest to make it stronger by absorbing other Fire-type's power. Ash is upset by Paul's attitude

TRAVEL TIP

The well-named Hearthome City has captured the hearts of many visitors — like Brock and Holly. Croagunk usually uses Poison Jab to cut off Brock's flirting, but since the feeling is mutual this time, it finally lets Brock keep the hearts in his eyes for Holly.

and lack of cooperation, but he refuses to let Paul cramp his style!

First up, Dawn, Piplup, Conway, and Slowking successfully defeat a Scyther and Koffining. Brock, Sudowoodo, Holly, and Wingull also win against a Bagon and Yanma.

When it's Ash and Paul's turn, Pikachu and Chimchar are up against a Magmar and Rhydon. While Paul sends Chimchar into the Lava Plume fire, Ash protects Pikachu. Then he borrows a move from Zoey to split Rhydon's surfing wave and win the round!

Unfortunately, Ash is so frustrated with Paul, he can't even enjoy their success. Will their poor teamwork put an end to their chances of winning the supersonic Soothe Bell, or will they get lucky again in Round Two?

CHIMCHAR

Type: Fire

Height: 1' 08"

Weight: 13.7 lbs

A Pokémon special to the Sinnoh Region, this playful Fire-type is full of fire. At the tip of its tail is a flame that runs on fuel from Chimchar's stomach. It is so strong, even raindrops can't put it out.

HEARTHOME CITY

Pokémon: Diamond and Pearl, Episode 50
Glory Blaze

Hearthome City is all abuzz as the second round of the Pokémon Tag-Team Battle is about to begin. Since Nurse Joy is short-staffed and swamped with Poké Balls, Brock offers to pitch in and help her heal all the Pokémon. Holly, his battle partner, is jealous of the attention Brock gives Joy, but is impressed with his ability to care for Pokémon.

While Paul is practicing with Chimchar, it accidentally strikes Ash with a powerful flash of fire. Ash doesn't get mad, since the attack was so impressive. However, he is worried about the way Paul pushes Chimchar. It looks so exhausted, Ash insists on taking Chimchar to the Pokémon Center to rest.

In the waiting room, Ash asks Paul why he is so hard on Chimchar. Paul tells him how they met after he was impressed by Chimchar's ability to fend off a group of Zangoose all by itself. Since that impressive battle, Paul has been trying to duplicate the stress of that situation to get Chimchar to perform another amazing fight.

Back at the contest, Paul and Chimchar are facing a fight with a Zangoose. Chimchar panics under the pressure and faints from fear. Ash and Pikachu step in and, together with Chimchar, they are able to defeat Zangoose and Metagross. While Paul ignores the Pokémon, Ash congratulates them for winning another rough round!

TRAVEL TIP

The Pokémon Center in Hearthome City gets overwhelmed around Tag-Team Battle time. So if you have a Pokémon that's all tuckered out, be sure to bring it in early!

Pokémon: Diamond and Pearl, Episode 51
Smells Like Team Spirit

Even after winning Round Two, Paul is still dissatisfied with Chimchar and sets it free. Ash and Turtwig ask Chimchar to join their family.

Before Ash can seal the deal, Team Rocket captures Chimchar. Ash vows to rescue Chimchar, and the Fire-type Pokémon is so touched by his caring new comrades that it bursts out of Team Rocket's robotic grasp. Chimchar runs right back to Ash, who catches in a Poké Ball.

TRAVEL TIP

Soothe Bells make sweet music. Before a battle, chime in with these silver bells to make your Pokémon happy-go-lucky.

The crew is ready for the third round of the Pokémon Competition! It's Brock, Holly, Croagunk, and Farfetch'd versus Ash, Staravia, Paul, and Torterra. However, Paul still refuses to play nicely, and he instructs Torterra to hit Staravia even though they're on the same team. Despite this, Ash and Paul still manage to beat Brock and Holly.

After the match, Brock tries to find Holly, but she's left town to start a quest to earn his love. Back at the battlegrounds, Ash, Paul, Chimchar, and Elekid are up against Dawn, her partner Conway, Buizel, and Heracross. During the fight, Elekid evolves into Electabuzz. By combining its moves with Chimchar, Ash and Paul win the final round!

Paul throws his reward at Ash and storms off.

Always looking for a new challenge, Ash and the crew head to Veilstone City, Paul's hometown.

TORTERRA

Type: Grass/Ground

Height: 7' 03" Weight: 683.4 lbs

Torterra is so huge, smaller Pokémon sometimes build nests on its back. When Torterra travel in groups, they have been mistaken for moving forests.

Who's Who in Sinnoh
New Friends

DAWN

Born and raised in Twinleaf Town, Dawn has just turned ten and begun her journey to become a Top Coordinator. As the daughter of a highly decorated Coordinator, Johanna, Dawn is dedicated to becoming one of the best. Dawn always makes sure she and her Pokémon are well groomed. This girlie go-getter is also a great friend to Brock and Ash as they travel through Sinnoh together.

Following in the footsteps of her grandfather, courageous Cheryl has dedicated her life to hunting treasure. With the help of a map, Mothim, and her new pals Ash, Dawn, and Brock, she finds a place her grandpop missed — the amazing Amber Castle.

CONWAY

Conway is always calculating! He has a way with numbers and Pokémon, like the Slowking, Heracross, and Aggron he has on hand. During the Tag-Team Battle in Hearthome City, he was Dawn's partner.

CHARACTER INDEX

Who's Who in Sinnoh
New Friends

HOLLY

Brock's beautiful partner in the Tag-Team Battle in Hearthome City may have met her match! Impressed by Brock's ability to battle and care for Pokémon, she was heartbroken after she and Brock lost the competition. But she vowed to improve with Wingull and Farfetch'd to impress Brock.

NANDO

This laidback singing sensation loves to make music and friends wherever he goes. Nando is both a Pokémon Coordinator and Trainer. Along with his Roselia, Kricketune, and Sunflora, he has been awarded the Eterna City Ribbon, the Hearthome City Ribbon, and the Forest Badge.

RHONDA

The host of the television show *Sinnoh Now*, Rhonda loves to chase stories. A true professional, she always keeps talking to the camera, even if it's just to yell at her crew when they hit her in the head with a microphone.

ZOEY

The competitive redheaded Coordinator is often up against Dawn at contests. Cool, friendly, and an all-around good sport, Zoey is always offering Dawn helpful advice and encouragement. Zoey already has two ribbons, including one from the Jubilife City Contest.

Who's Who in Sinnoh
Gym Leaders

GARDENIA

The Eterna City Gym Leader

A Grass-type fanatic, Gardenia protects all the Pokémon in the Eterna Forest and is responsible for awarding the Forest Badge. Her loyal messenger, Nuzleaf, alerts her to trouble. She always travels with trusty Cherubi, Roserade, and Turtwig.

ROARK

Oreburgh City Gym Leader

Roark is obsessed with Rock-types. The keeper of the Coal Badge cares for a Rampardos, Onix, and Geodude. In his spare time, Roark digs deep for fossils in local mines and then generously donates his discoveries to the Oreburgh City Museum.

Who's Who in Sinnoh Advisors

A former Top Coordinator, Dawn's mother encourages her daughter to be independent and follow her dreams. Her Glameow always stays by her side at home.

Super smart and friendly, Professor Rowan is a top Pokémon researcher. From his lab in Sandgem Town, he gives out Pokémon and studies local Pokémon and their Evolution. You can always call on Professor Rowan if you have a question.

Who's Who in Sinnoh
Inspirational Heroes

CYNTHIA

The Pokémon League Champion of Sinnoh, Cynthia is very interested in the Legendary Pokémon of space and time, Dialga and Palkia. Cynthia has dedicated her life to discovering the truth behind the mysterious Pokémon origins. Cynthia is a caring person, but with Garchomp, she's also a force to be reckoned with on the battlefield.

Longhaired Lucian is one of the members of Sinnoh's Elite Four. The Psychic-type expert Trainer is a sharp dresser with an even sharper mind. He is always seen wearing his signature suit and purple-tinted glasses. Together with his buddy Bronzong, Lucian is unstoppable.

CHARACTER INDEX

Who's Who in Sinnoh Rivals

KENNY

Dawn's foe from childhood and a fellow Coordinator, Kenny bumps into Dawn at the Floaroma Town Contest. He annoys her by bragging about his experiences, telling embarrassing stories, and calling Dawn by her babyish nickname, Dee Dee. Personality differences aside, Kenny is a skilled Coordinator who cares for Alakazam, Breloom, and Prinplup.

PAUL

An arrogant Trainer, Paul is Ash's rival in Sinnoh. While impatient Paul has been awarded the Coal Badge and many others, he doesn't work hard practicing. He is only interested in having the strongest Pokémon and constantly abandons the ones he captures if they're not the best or if they disappoint him during battle. Paul is a bad sport who could care less about making friends.

CHARACTER INDEX

Who's Who in Sinnoh
Sinnoh's Most Wanted

POKÉMON HUNTER J

High-tech thief Hunter J will swoop in on Salamence, steal your Pokémon, and then sell it to the highest bidder. Aided by a flying tank full of goons, J is always on the prowl for Pokémon. And she's always ready to pick a fight.

HUNTER J

GOON

TEAM ROCKET
Keep your eyes peeled for a triple dose of trouble! With Jesse, James, and Meowth on the loose, you never know where they'll show up next. Team Rocket has a new motto and some new outfits, so turn the page to check out the new costumes they've been seen sneaking around in.
JESSE
JAMES
MEOWTH

Who's Who in Sinnoh
Sinnoh's Most Wanted

TEAM ROCKET IN DISGUISE

GYM LEADER, PRINCESS POWER ZONE JESSE

HOTELIERS

JESSE AS A COWGIRL
JAMES AS JAMESON

CLOWNS GIVING AWAY POKETCHS

JUDGES

BUSINESS PEOPLE

ROCK CLIMBERS

MINERS

THE COMBEE WATERFALL

Deep within the Eterna Forest is a patch of Pomeg flowers. If you follow the Combee from the garden back to their colony, they'll lead you to a tall waterfall filled with Bug-and-Flying-types. If you go even further, behind the falls, you'll find the infamous Wall of Combee and the Amber Castle where Vespiquen lives.

THE THOUSAND-YEAR-OLD TREE

In the unspoiled woods of Sinnoh, a tremendous tree has been growing strong for 1,000 years. A huge colony of Seedot, Nuzleaf, and Shiftry call its shady branches home.

VALLEY PATH

Protected by preserve ranger Rosebay, the Valley Path is a great place to find Sinnoh's finest Flying-types, like Pidgeot and Hoothoot.

BEWILDER FOREST

Home to hundreds of hypnotizing wild Stantler, this dark forest is famous for trapping trainers as they try to travel through. It's easy to get caught in a Stantler's gaze and get sent to dreamland, which makes getting out a nightmare!

OREBURGH CITY MINE

If you're interested in ancient Pokémon, this place is a must-see! Often excavated by Pokémon paleontologists like Gym Leader Roark, the Oreburgh City Mine site is full of rock-solid finds.

STONE MAZE

Towering blocks of solid stone make up the twists and turns of this ancient landmark. While the cave entrance is hard to find, once you're there it's even easier to get lost inside. Climb to the top of the pyramid to find flowering trees and a clear view of how to head out.

AMBER PALACE

It takes a true explorer to find this treasure made of treats hidden behind a waterfall, deep within a cave, beyond a crystal hallway. The golden castle shimmers with the Enchanted Honey that makes up its walls and overflows from giant cups. Cared for by thousands of Combee and their lovely leader, Vespiquen, the palace is as beautiful as it is delicious.

POKÉMON NATURE PRESERVE

Between Eterna City and Hearthome Town is a natural habitat for rare Pokémon that is guarded by Professor Oak's nephew, Gary. Be sure to bring your binoculars to spot the many Pokémon who call the preserve home.

OREBURGH SCIENTIFIC CENTER

This museum and research center gets its fossils from local mines. While the stone specimens alone are impressive, many ancient Pokémon have been brought back to life through the research lab's hi-tech fossil restorers.

TOP FIVE BATTLES IN SINNOH

5

Cynthia vs. Paul

While visiting the sacred shrine to the Legendary Pokémon Dialga and Palkia, Paul obnoxiously challenges Cynthia, the Pokémon League Champion of Sinnoh, to a big six Pokémon Battle. He is booed by the audience and ends the battle early when Cynthia's Garchomp easily defeats Chimchar, Weavile, Murkrow, and Torterra. Cynthia sure taught Paul a lesson or two.

4

Ash and Dawn vs. the Champ Twins

At the request of Rhonda the reporter, Ash and Dawn challenge the undefeated Champ Twins. During their first Tag-Team Battle together, Dawn and Ash mostly fought each other and got badly beaten — just like the sixteen trainers before them. After talking out their differences and deciding to use teamwork as their main strategy, Dawn, Ash, Piplup, and Turtwig win their second match against their renowned competitors Brian, Ryan, Croconaw, and Quilava.

3

Ash vs. Cynthia and Dawn vs. Johanna

While these imaginary battles may have been caused by a menacing Mismagius, they certainly fulfilled everyone's dreams. Brock sat in the stands surrounded by adoring ladies, Ash was awarded every badge, and Dawn won all the ribbons from every region. It may have turned into a nightmare in the end, but the fantasy was still fun!

2

Dawn vs. Kenny at the Floaroma Contest

On the contest battlefield, Dawn shows her childhood rival how strong she's become as a person and a Pokémon Coordinator. In the final round, she and Piplup beat Kenny and the evolved form of Piplup, Prinplup, with their magnificent new move, Whirlpool. The remarkable win earns Dawn her first contest ribbon.

1

Ash's Rematch with Roark

Although he was initially defeated by Roark and his unstoppable Cranidos, when the Rock-type evolves into an even tougher competitor, Rampardos, Ash asks Roark to have another go in the gym rink. Using clever moves he practiced with Brock, Ash has a surprisingly good showing with Turtwig. Together, they win Ash's first gym battle in Sinnoh and the coveted Coal Badge.

NEW POKÉMON PALS

ASH

STARLY/STARAVIA

With Brock's help, Ash captures a Starly he spots in the sky to help him find Pikachu, who was stolen by Team Rocket the second Ash arrived in Sinnoh. Well cared for by his new pal, Starly soon evolves into Staravia during a fight to save its fellow Flying-types at the Valley Path.

TURTWIG

This tough Turtwig protects all the Pokémon in the area, but after meeting Ash it asks to join him on his journey. Impressed by Turtwig's strength and compassion, Ash agrees take it along with him.

CHIMCHAR

When Paul abandons this poor Pokémon in Hearthome City, Ash is there with open arms. Happy to have a friendly new family, Chimchar fits right in as it fights off Team Rocket!

BROCK

CROAGUNK

Croagunk sees Meowth at the supermarket and follows it back to meet Team Rocket. While they could care less about the Poison-and-Fighting-type type Pokémon, Brock meets and befriends Croagunk and offers to take care of it.

HAPPINY

With the help of Croagunk, who made a convincing Politoed at the Pokémon Dress-Up Contest, Brock is awarded a Pokémon Egg. When it hatches, an adorable Happiny makes Brock proud.

PIPLUP

After fending off wild Ariados together, Dawn picks the Piplup from Professor Rowan's lab to be her Pokémon pal!

BUNEARY

Although Pikachu initially caught Buneary's eye, Dawn and Piplup were able to capture their furry friend after fighting off Team Rocket together.

PACHIRISU

Dawn passes the Electric-type while on path to Floaroma Town. She instantly falls in love with the little blue furball, but it keeps zapping her until her hair stands on end. When Dawn tries to abandon it on account of its bad behavior, Jesse goes after Pachirisu. Then the Electric-type Pokémon puts up a good fight to stay with its friend Dawn!

BUIZEL

This Water-type likes to put up a fight! It had defeated so many trainers, Ash, Zoey, and Dawn all decided they had to try to catch it. Even after all three lost battle afte battle to the undefeated Buizel, it still kept challenging them. Finally, Dawn and Piplup succee in catching it with a BubbleBeam Whirlpool combination.

THE JOURNEY ISN'T OVER YET!

When Ash first arrived in Sinnoh, he was seeking a new set of adventures, but he had no idea how much fun he would have — or how far he would go! After bumping into his buddy Brock and meeting a Coordinator called Dawn, they united to form a cool and courageous traveling crew.

From their start in Sandgem Town, through Bewilder Forest, an Aerodactyl attack, Team Rocket's tricks, a stone maze, and a stormy blackout, Ash, Dawn, and Brock went through many trials and have come out triumphant. So far Ash has earned two badges, Dawn got her first Pokémon and first ribbon, and Brock won an Egg that hatched a baby Happiny.

As our heroes head on to Veilstone City, more challenges, pals, and Pokémon await them just on the other side of Sinnoh.